Broken

BREAKING THE RULES SERIES

Annette,
  Enjoy the series!
    XOXO
    K Webster

K. Webster

Dedication

Grandmother, you encouraged my love for reading very early on in my life and I will forever be grateful for you showing me how to escape a terrible world and dive in to a wonderful one without ever having to leave my seat.

Prologue

5 months earlier…

We were dead. Not a soul had walked into the café for the last two hours, which was completely insane for New York City. The Taylor Swift concert in Central Park had completely stolen away all of our patrons. Bored to tears, I scrolled through my phone, looking at pictures of me and Brayden.

Brayden was the love of my life. We met our first year at Columbia in Freshman Comp. His messy blond hair and crystal blue eyes had captivated me from the moment he sat down beside me. We had started out as friends but quickly morphed into lovers. He stole my breath every time I saw him. *Even to this day.*

Bray was at Columbia on a baseball scholarship, studying Architecture like me. Now that graduation was just two weeks away, we'd be able to start focusing on the rest of our lives. A few months ago, on Valentine's Day, he proposed to me in Central Park. It was terribly cliché and romantic. Of course now, instead of focusing on finals, I could only think of my upcoming wedding and becoming the future Mrs. Brayden Greene.

I stopped on a recent picture of us after a baseball game. We were so happy, smiling back in the photo. *The All-American couple.* I thought this picture would be the perfect one for our engagement announcement that was going to go in the newspaper soon.

Dragging me out of my daydreaming, my boss Jeanie hollered at me. "Honey, you might as well go home. I can't afford for us to be this slow and pay you to drool over your fiancé. Think of it as your engagement present. Your one and only day to ever get out early. You can thank Taylor Swift."

Completely excited over the news because I never got to leave early, I ran over and pulled the gruff woman into a hug. "Thank you, Jeanie!" I exclaimed. Pushing me away with a grunt, she said, "Well, go before I change my mind, little lady. And don't get any ideas about this happening again." *Thank you, Taylor Swift.*

Bray and I hardly ever got to spend evenings together because of my job at the café and his playing baseball. This evening I was going to surprise him. Give him a taste of what a good wife I could be. He was going to love what I planned on doing to him once I got hold of his sexy body.

Practically skipping the two blocks to my dorm, I rushed into my room and changed out of my uniform. I put on my new black lingerie that I'd been dying to show him and stopped to admire myself in the mirror. *Heels.* I needed heels to complete the look. Just as I slipped them on, the door flung open, revealing my roommate Pepper.

"What the hell, Andi!" she screeched covering her eyes as she made a beeline to her desk.

"I got out of work early and I'm going to surprise Bray," I told her, smiling. Even with her back to me, I could tell she was rolling her eyes. Pepper was an adorable girl, but she hid behind her glasses, Columbia sweatshirts, and messy buns. She was one of the most intelligent people I had ever met.

Having been placed together as dorm mates, we instantly

became the best of friends. I was the sweet, innocent girl in love with a baseball player. She was the Victoria's Secret model dressed as a nerd with a little—*okay, a lot*—of attitude. We came from different worlds and liked different things but meshed incredibly well.

"Are you going to prance on over to his room dressed like a hooker?" she asked in her sardonic tone.

Now it was my turn to roll my eyes. "No way! I'm going to wear my coat. He won't know what hit him," I laughed. She tried to sound annoyed with me, but Pepper was in no way immune to my happy-girl charms and let out a chuckle.

Wrapping up in my jacket, I blew her a kiss as I walked out the door. Bray wouldn't be expecting me for few more hours so he was going to be shocked when he saw me. He told me he'd be studying for finals in his room while I was working, so I knew he'd be there. And if his roommate Josh was there, I was going to tell him to get lost. I missed Bray and I wanted to have some hot sex with my fiancé. *Fiancé.* I still couldn't get used to the idea.

When I got to his room, I quietly opened it, wanting to surprise him. Realizing that the lights were off and that he might be napping, I decided I was going to hop into bed with him and *really* surprise my man. That was until I heard the moan. *What in the world is he doing over there?*

Hesitantly, I fumbled for the switch. My eyes froze in horror at the scene before me. A naked girl—with really big boobs—was bouncing on MY naked Brayden. *What?* I was having trouble processing how a naked girl was with MY fiancé.

Everything went in slow motion at that point. The girl jumped up, scrambling for clothes. Brayden asked me what I was doing there while covering himself with the blanket. I was backing out of the room, tears wickedly streaming. He called after me as I ran away. The man had effectively smashed my heart to pieces.

The trip back to my room was a blur. Once I burst through our door, I met Pepper's eyes. She instantly held her arms open to me, and I ran into them.

"Brayden is a bastard," she whispered, stroking my hair, knowing without words what had happened. My life was ruined. This happy girl would no longer ever be happy.

Chapter ONE

Present

"Come on, Andi! I don't have all day. Some of us have been ready for hours," Pepper called to me from the living room. Of course she'd been ready for hours. She was wearing jeans and a sweater for crying out loud, and it probably took two minutes to readjust her bun.

"Perfection takes time," I told Olive, who was sitting on my bed while I applied the last of my makeup. "You sure you don't want to go with us, hon?" I asked, turning to look at her. Olive was our new friend. She was a gorgeous black girl with legs that went on for miles. Her hair was smooth as silk and her eyes were the palest orbs that contrasted vividly against her chocolate skin.

Olive moved in with us about a month ago. She somehow managed to escape an extremely abusive relationship but had nowhere to go. When I found her crying at the café one day, I took her under my wing, praying Pepper would be okay with it. Of course Pepper fell in love with the leggy chocolate goddess as well, and she'd been living with us ever since.

Olive got modeling gigs left and right because she was perfection personified. But her fears of her ex sometimes cripple her socially. *A lot of times.* Like tonight, she was adamantly shaking her head to my offer. She had a fear that she might run into Drake and he'd drag her away from us, never to be seen again. It always gave me the shivers to think about what he must have done to her to make her so afraid. And the fact that she refused to ever let us see her without being fully clothed made me wonder if he'd done something to her body. Just the thought made me sick to my stomach.

The modeling jobs she took were mostly for magazines. She absolutely refused to do any live modeling at shows even though that would have been the best way for her to get noticed by more well-known agents. Olive gave us money when she got paid on these jobs, but we never asked her for any. We just wanted our girl safe with us.

I didn't make much money at the café so Pepper was our breadwinner. Well, if you call having a monthly trust fund "breadwinning" then she was definitely it. Her dad was a high-powered attorney there in the city and didn't want his little girl to hurt for anything. We lived in a sweet little apartment and didn't hurt for much either thanks to Pepper being "Daddy's Little Girl." Oh, and she played the part so well. The girl could be downright bitchy, but when—Daddy—was around, her voice was as sweet as sugar.

Thankfully, I was going to start my new job on Monday and would be able to help Pepper out more than just buying the groceries. Even though her dad took care of a lot for us, I still felt guilty about being a total freeloader. Today was my last day at the café and now we were going to celebrate. It took several months after college of applying all over the city to finally land a job at Compton Enterprises. The job I really wanted was to be an architect, but working as an assistant at an architectural firm was a good foot in the door. Everyone has to start somewhere.

"One day I'll go with you guys. But it's just too soon. Please have fun for me. I have a date with American Idol," she smiled at me.

"Okay, fine. But I'm holding you to it. Now, how do I look?" I asked her, flipping my hair over my shoulder.

Ever since the day I found Brayden cheating on me, something in me snapped. Gone was the blond-haired innocent. Gone was my optimism. My outlook on life and love had been ruined the moment I saw that girl's big tits bouncing as she rode my man. He had stolen it all away from me when he decided to sleep with some bimbo after almost four years of dating.

Now, I was this hard, jaded woman. Away had gone my conservative ways and I had welcomed my inner skank. I glanced at my reflection in the full-length mirror on the wall. My platinum-blond hair was flat-ironed perfectly straight halfway down my back. I had carefully made up my face, complete with smoky eyes and plump red lips. The dress I chose to wear was black, tight, and short. Just the way I liked it. The plunging neckline revealed my adequate cleavage. My red pumps put me up three inches higher than my five foot seven frame.

"You look beautiful as always, Andi," Olive genuinely assured, making me smile at her.

I was in "Man-Killer Mode" as Pepper called it. I'd have them falling at my feet tonight. One of them would get lucky too. I was on the prowl, and even Pepper wouldn't be able to tame me. This Friday night was about to get crazy.

"Thanks, babe. See you in the morning," I waved to her as I grabbed my clutch and walked out my bedroom door. Pepper was curled up in the recliner reading a book. "Let's go, bitch," I told her as I shrugged into my coat.

"About time, bitch," she shot at me, picking up hers from the back of the chair as she stood up. *Man-Killer Mode: Activated.*

A DARK TWO WEEKS...

Today, I am absolutely sick to my stomach. Not eating hardly anything for several days straight has sent my body into a tailspin. My head throbs, I'm weak, my body hurts, and now I am throwing up. Pepper told me earlier that things were getting out of control, that she was going to drag me out of the bed if I didn't get my act together soon. I just flipped her off and threw the covers over my head.

Thankfully, I was caught up on all of my classes before the "incident." I was really just waiting to take my finals. I have worked my ass off for four years. Surely I can take the week off without catching flak from Pepper. Wishful thinking.

My heart still hurts so fucking bad. I keep playing reruns over and over again of "what-ifs". Every scenario ends the same. Bray is a cheater. He even had the nerve to come to my dorm room, but luckily Pepper ran interference.

Hearing his voice successfully caused me to break down all over again. He was begging her. She was cussing him out. I was sobbing uncontrollably.

Will it ever get better? I'll never be able to love or trust again. Brayden was it for me. Now I have nothing.

Chapter TWO

The cab ride only took ten minutes since the new bar we wanted to go to was just a few blocks away. On the way there, I thought about how my life had gone from spending every weekend with my fiancé to sleeping with a different guy each weekend instead. Since Bray had left me a broken mess with his infidelity, I woke up one morning needing a different way to live. The way I could cope was to sleep around with successful, hot men and drop them before either of us could get invested emotionally. It made for exciting weekends full of free dinners and lots of unattached sex.

In the last five months, I had morphed into this succubus—taking their energy and keeping it for my own. And I loved every minute of it. Unfortunately, there were always the guys who would seem genuinely hurt when the weekend was over. Thus—our little escapades would effectively be over too. Somehow I was a bitch and a whore even though the little shits knew from the get-go what to expect. Pepper said that I needed help. I thought I was doing just fine. My heart never hurt anymore, that's for damn sure.

Once we had graduated and moved into Pepper's apartment,

she had gotten a job at the museum as an assistant production manager. Her degree was actually being put to some use. I was still whipping up lattes and running out deli sandwiches to a busy crowd. Finally, though, things were looking up, because I had successfully ended my last day at the café today and would embark on my future on Monday. My interview had gone great at Compton Enterprises. The owner of the company, Jordan Compton, was who I would be assisting. He'd told me that the ability to advance at the company was available if I were willing to work for it. I was eager to finally start my career after all these months since graduation.

When the cab stopped, I paid the driver and we got out. For a moment, we drank in the atmosphere of the new bar. Dempsey's was glowing above the entrance in red—promising a new tantalizing adventure. I'd heard that it was an Irish pub-like bar that was modern and cool. They'd only been open a few weeks and had already hosted some great local bands. Tonight, a new local favorite, The Remains, were supposed to be playing.

When I walked to the entrance, the meaty-looking guy checked our IDs and grumbled, "Twenty-dollar cover each."

"What the fuck?" Pepper exclaimed. "Twenty dollars just to let me in the door and then I still have to pay you to drink the damn alcohol?" She was glaring at him, pissed at the overpriced cover fee.

Just as I was about to tell Pepper to chill out, another man whispered into Meathead's ear, causing him to frown. "Nevermind. You've been paid for," he muttered gruffly, stepping aside so we could pass. I looked down at my very naked, very long legs. *Score one for Andi.* Smiling at Meathead, we entered the bar.

The smells instantly intoxicated me as we walked in. The mix of smoke, lager, and an oaky smell permeated my senses. Clearly the band hadn't come on yet because all that could be heard was the dull roar of people talking. The bar was quite spacious, and it exuded richness. The tables and barstools all were dark mahogany. I looked around and noticed that the walls were lined in mahogany paneling from floor to ceiling. I almost thought this place could be a library at a really rich person's house.

Grabbing Pepper's hand, I walked her over to the bar so we could get drinks. The many hungry stares as we passed didn't go unnoticed, and I shivered at how it excited me. Knowing that I could have whatever man I wanted in here made me feel powerful. I'd be fucking one of these poor souls in just a few hours. I smiled as I scanned the crowd.

When we got to the bar, I squeezed between two barstools so I could tell the bartender our order. When he came over, I drank in his piercings, tattoos, and Irish accent.

"What can I get you two lovely ladies?"

"I'll have a Cosmopolitan and a Cape Cod," I told him. He winked at me and went over to make our drinks. He was pretty good-looking, but if I ever wanted to come back to this bar again, I'd have to pass this one up.

"When do The Remains come on?" Pepper asked, looking over at the empty stage.

"In fifteen minutes," the gravelly voiced bartender told us as he handed us our drinks. I pulled out a twenty to pay for our drinks, but he held up a hand, stopping me. "Ladies, I would pretty much say every drink you want for the rest of the night will be free. I just had several different guys say that they wanted to buy your drinks," he laughed.

I smiled and thanked him before Pepper and I made our way to the stage. We sat at a tall table near the stage as two people vacated it. Pepper pushed the still smoking ashtray away from us and brought her Cape Cod to her lips to take a sip. "This place is nice, Andi. I'm glad we came. However, I kind of feel like we're at a meat market and we're big, juicy steaks," she reported, snidely rolling her eyes at the guys a table over who were blatantly ogling us.

"Pepper, just enjoy the free drinks and attention. We'll find some nice guys to take home later," I teased, winking at her. She just stuck her tongue at me. I liked to mess with her, knowing that she would not, in fact, be taking a guy home. Pepper didn't warm up to people very easily. Olive and I were probably her only friends of either sex. She was serious and bitchy. I loved it about her, but others couldn't handle it. For as long as I'd known Pepper, she'd never dated anyone at all. If I had to guess, I'd bet she was still a virgin. And quite honestly, I thought she had a hard time finding people that could match her intellectual wit. They only bored her when they came up short.

"Hello, ladies," a blond-haired guy in a tight t-shirt greeted as he walked up to our table. He had a cute face and he looked pretty buff. This might work.

"Well, hello yourself," I purred as I leaned forward, giving him a straight view down my cleavage. His eyes widened as he stepped closer to enjoy the view from a better vantage point. Pepper's sigh could be heard nearby.

"What are two beautiful ladies doing sitting here all alone?" he asked, laying down his cheesy pick-up line. I winced—only slightly—because it was already turning me off. But sex was sex. As long as I kept his mouth occupied with other things, I could avoid the things that might come out of it.

Clearly already annoyed, Pepper huffed out, "I'm going to the bathroom." She stormed off, leaving me with Blondie.

"Have a seat, good-looking," I drawled out, matching his cheesiness. He grinned back at me with his perfect white teeth and sat down.

"A woman, like yourself, and I could have a damn good time, if you know what I mean," he suggested, promising a good fuck.

I took a long sip of my drink and looked up at him under my eyelashes. "Is that so, handsome? Well, then by all means, I'd like to see what you mean."

He shifted in his chair, clearly excited at my answer. "Well let's get out of here, beautiful," he suggested, smiling.

"Okay, we can get right to it. But we need to go over the rules first," I declared, voice matter of fact, as I went into business mode. He sat back in his chair, looking at me questioningly. "First of all, it's just fucking. Nothing more. Secondly, you get three nights of it. Just three. Friday. Saturday. Sunday. You will love every second of it. After we're finished on the third night, you go away. Done. It's simple and easy. Are you game?"

His eyes had grown to the size of saucers as he just stared at me, open-mouthed and shocked that a woman would insinuate such a proposition.

Rolling my eyes, already getting bored, I asked him one more time, "Are you game? Do you want to play by my rules?" He glanced up behind me and slid out of his chair, stalking off. *What the hell?* Loser. He couldn't handle what I had to give anyway.

Before I could start searching out my next victim, I felt the heat of someone's body leaning behind me. The deep voice that whispered hot breath into my ear sent a shockwave right down to my core when he said, "I want to play."

I shuddered at the sheer sexiness of his growled words. *Please let this one be hot, I thought, because I could almost just get off on his voice alone.* "Is that so? You think my game sounds fun?" I solicited, egging him on but still not turning around to see him. A big, masculine hand snaked around me and settled on my upper thigh, rubbing a thumb just under the hemline of my dress. My body shivered with need as I realized just how close his thumb was to the aching, throbbing part of me in my really short dress.

I dropped my head to the side, allowing my hair to cascade behind me giving him full access to my neck. *My bait.* And just like the good little player I knew he would be, he brushed his lips up my neck to just under my ear, where he pecked me, short and sweet. Between his lips on my neck and the thumb running a delicious pattern just under my dress, I was ready for him to throw me across the table and fuck me like nobody else was in the room.

About that moment, I saw Pepper walking back toward the table, glaring at my overt sexuality. Before she reached the table, the voice whispered, "Don't go anywhere. I'll find you again in a bit. We have a game to play." And as quickly as he had appeared, he disappeared.

"What the fuck, Andi? You looked like you were about two seconds away from letting Mr. Tall, Dark, and Handsome finger you in the fucking bar!" she shouted at me. Slowly coming out of my sexual haze, I spun around to look for him. There was nothing but a large crowd building around the stage. No Mr. Tall, Dark, and Handsome.

"Pepper, I am going to fuck the shit out that man tonight," I told her dreamily. Mr. Tall, Dark, and Handsome dripped with sexuality and I wanted to drink it up. At this point, even if he was ugly, I'd just have him do me from behind. *What?*

Before she could scold me anymore, we were interrupted by the sound of a guitar. The Remains had finally taken stage. A waitress stopped at our table and dropped off two more drinks for us. "These are compliments of Jackson," she said to me like I should have known who that was. After we thanked her, we sat back to enjoy the show.

"Thanks Jackson!" Pepper and I giggled to each other.

The Remains were amazing. They were a local band that had the edginess of old '90s grunge bands but swoon-worthy lyrics that I'd expected to hear from more recent bands. The crowd was wild for them. After an hour of playing, they finally said their goodbyes and left the stage.

"That was awesome!" Pepper told me, no longer pissed at me.

"I'm going to go to the ladies' room. Get us another round of drinks," I ordered as I strode away from the table. Being a thin blonde who was scantily clad, I was used to the stares of men all around. I drank it up because it did miracles for my self-esteem that Bray had managed to damage.

Before I reached the hallway to the restrooms, I felt *his* eyes on me. *Mr. Tall, Dark, and Handsome.* I scanned the area to see if I could pick him out from the crowd. Not seeing him anywhere, I tossed my hair back and breezed into the bathroom. I couldn't wait for my little player to find me so we could start our game. This was the first time I had actually found excitement in my game to this degree. Sure, it was fun and carefree, but something about his voice had promised a lot more than just fun. I couldn't wait.

I walked out of the bathroom and down the hallway but stopped to look at a picture on the wall. It was absolutely gorgeous, a stunning collection of buildings with clean lines and asymmetrical perfection. The photographer had captured the beauty of the buildings. My architectural mind wanted to continue to appreciate it, but a voice behind me ripped me away from those thoughts.

"It's called the Poustinia. It won The Royal Institute of the Architects of Ireland's trennial gold medal in 2004-2006," the smooth voice educated me. *Mr. Tall, Dark, and Handsome.* Between his sexy voice and his knowledge of architecture, I nearly begged him to do naughty things to me right then and there. "Close your eyes," he said, grabbing my hand.

Closing them, I allowed him to lead me down the hallway away from the bar toward the room that boasted an "Employees Only" sign I had noticed on my way to the bathroom.

"Do you work here?" I asked him, eyes still pressed shut. His deep chuckle had me clenching my thighs together.

"I'm friends with the owner. But don't tell him what we're about to do on his desk," he added conspiratorially.

I sighed at his words, nodding as he pulled me through the door, and closed it behind us. "Are you ready to start our game?" he growled into my ear, sending shivers of need down my spine.

"Yes. Can I open my eyes now?"

"Hmmm. There's just something really fucking sexy about you not being able to see my face. I don't want you to see me till after I make you come. You like that rule?" he inquired, clearly making up his own rules as we went along.

"What if you look like a dog? Kind of unfair to let me fuck

you only to find out you are ugly," I told him snootily, hoping to egg him on.

He pulled my back to him so I could feel his hardness against my back. I gasped when I felt the very large size of it. His hands slid around my body, settling on my tummy as he whispered his hot breath into my ear. "I've never had any complaints," he bragged, nudging his hardness into me a little.

My body shuddered because I wanted him right now. I didn't care what he looked like. I was going to fuck his voice.

Reading my mind, he pushed us forward until my thighs met what I presumed was the desk. Not gently at all, he bent me over so that my arms were spread across the desk, knocking papers off in the process. He nudged my bottom with his hard cock through our clothes, making me whimper because I wanted it so badly.

"So three days. We're agreeing to just three days, right? I can't start this game without knowing that we both fully understand the rules," he said in a very businesslike manner, as if he was going over a contract.

"Yes. That's how the game is played. We get to be each other's plaything for a whole weekend and then we can go back to our lives come the start of the week. Are you going to fuck me or not?" I demanded testily, ready for him to plow into me.

Not saying another word, I heard the jingle of his belt and the sound of his pants falling to the ground. I shivered with excitement. Slowly, he eased my short dress up over my hips and grabbed a handful of my ass.

"Woman, you are sexy as hell," he growled, once again rubbing himself against me. This time, the friction of his naked hardness against my thin thong had me shuddering. I was so wet and he hadn't even touched my clit.

He hooked his thumbs in my thong and slid it down my legs, letting it rest at my ankles. I heard the ripping of a condom package and my pussy began to throb.

"Oh my God, I can't wait any longer. Please, just fuck me

already!" I exclaimed eagerly, wanting him inside me. Not waiting for any more commands, he spread my sex and teased the entrance with his tip. I pressed backward to him, begging him to push it in. Finally, he groaned and shoved it all the way in, causing me to yelp out in delight.

My body took a moment to accept his size but then began clenching, wanting him to continue. He quickly started pounding into me. His hand came around and found my clit. As he thrust into me, he began a rhythmic pattern on my swollen nub that was quickly sending me toward the stars.

"Oh my God, I'm about to come," I shrieked as he continued to work me over. Within moments, my climax took over and I shuddered around his throbbing cock. He grunted, and I could feel his own climax course through him. He collapsed on top of me, his heart pounding against my back. Inhaling the sent of my hair, he said, "What's your name, sexy?"

"Andi. And that was amazing, Mr. Whoever You Are," I praised, short on breath.

His loud chuckle vibrated through me, causing me to begin to throb again for him. "Jackson. And that was really fucking amazing," he agreed.

I smiled, finally looking around to notice all the papers we'd shoved off the desk. *Oops.*

He lifted back off of me and slid out, involuntarily causing me to tremble at the loss. I could hear him pull his pants back up behind me and drop something into a trashcan—the condom I presumed. Stepping back behind me, he reached under me and pulled me up off the desk. His hands grabbed my dress and pulled it back down over my ass. Sighing, I started to bend to pull up my thong, but he stopped me by squatting behind me. Instead of pulling them back up, I saw his big hands lift my feet up to completely remove them.

"My prize," he laughed.

Finally, I couldn't stand it any longer. I needed to see the face of my lover. Spinning around before he could stop me, I drank in his beauty. He was stuffing my panties into his expensive suit pocket. When his brown eyes met mine, my knees weakened a bit. *Oh my God. Tall, dark, and handsome was the understatement of the year, Pepper.* This man was a god. His longish dark brown hair was perfectly styled on his head, making him look very GQ. Chocolate brown eyes studied mine as I greedily looked him over. The five-o' clock shadow on his face was sexy as hell. And his lips. God, I couldn't wait to put mine on them. The nice suit showcased a very tall, fit man.

Suddenly dragging me out of my thoughts, he uttered, "Like what you see?"

His cockiness caused me to roll my eyes at him. "I guess you'll do," I shot back at him, matching his tone. He arched an eyebrow and his laughter boomed in the office.

"You really are something, Andi. I'm going to enjoy playing our little game," he growled. He quickly leaned over and brushed his lips against mine but never gave into the full-on kiss I knew we both wanted. Pulling away as fast as he swooped in, he instructed, "Go to your friend. I will come get you in a little while and we can get on to the next round at my place."

Winking at him, I tossed my hair back and strode out of the room, not giving him the satisfaction of an answer. Tonight was off to a *great* start.

A DARK TWO WEEKS…

Today I finally dragged myself out of bed and showered. Even I was offended by my smell. Pepper told me that I should be using my time to study for my finals next week. Quite honestly, I could care less about them.

Bray texted me again today, once again begging me to forgive him. It wouldn't be so hard if he would just go away. But no. No, he needed me back because he suddenly "realized what a mistake I made." Too fucking bad, Bray.

Curious while in the bathroom, I weighed myself only to discover I've lost ten pounds. Oops. I'm not going to tell Pepper about that one.

How am I going to recover from this? I don't feel like this hole in my heart will ever close up. It feels as if I've been cut and am bleeding internally. I wish there were a way to numb my pain. How do people get over having their hearts ripped to shreds? I honestly have no idea how to stop the pain.

Chapter THREE

"Did you fall in?" Pepper asked, smirking when I walked up to our table.

"Oh Pepper, you have no idea how happy I am right now. Mr. Tall, Dark, and Handsome is named Jackson. He and I just had the hottest freaking quickie in the backroom," I exclaimed and started to laugh when she made a face.

"Andi! Are there any bounds to your sexcapades?" she frowned at me.

"Pepper, don't be jealous. That sexy man just banged the hell out of me over the desk and stole my panties. Dare I say he's a keeper?"

"So he's the new weekender I'm guessing?" she inquired, picking at her nail.

I sighed as I took a sip of my drink. "Yes, he's the new weekender. Don't worry though. We're going to his place. You can sleep peacefully tonight, my friend." She looked up at me with concerned eyes.

"Andi, I don't know if that's a good idea. It isn't safe to just run off with a perfect stranger you met in a bar, you know."

"Pepper, please. It will be fine. He is a nice businessman, looks really successful, knows about architecture. It's not a big deal. I promise," I assured her calmly.

She sighed as she conceded finally. Smiling, I grabbed her hand. Pepper was a great friend. Always concerned and looking out for me. I loved that girl. Putting on her bitch face, she shot out, "Now, don't get any STDs or pregnant. I swear, Andi, your vag is going to fall out one day!" Giggling, I kicked her under the table.

After a couple more drinks, she hopped off her stool and gave me a hug. "Andi, I am getting out of here and grabbing a cab home. Mr. Tall, Dark, and Handsome has been looking at you for the last fifteen minutes like he wants to devour you and it's making me kind of nauseous. Be safe and call me if you have problems. Love you, babe," she waved goodbye as she headed out of the bar.

As I watched her leave, an arm snaked around my shoulder. Smiling, I turned to say something sassy to Jackson but frowned when I realized it was just some guy who thought he had ownership over me now that my friend was gone. *Hell no.* Before I could rip his balls off with my words, he was jerked away from me.

"She's mine tonight, buddy," Jackson growled from behind me.

I laughed at his bold words. *Actually, I believe he is mine tonight.*

"You ready, Andi?" he questioned, pulling my hand into his.

"Why yes, Jackson. I'm ready to continue our delicious game," I confirm, looking into those dark eyes. They darted to my lips momentarily, so I licked them for good measure. Immediately his eyes met mine again.

"I think I've finally met my match," he growled, pulling me towards the exit. I smiled, thinking about how I'd affected this man. A man who looked like he led powerful meetings and had an army of employees under him. It was empowering when I could get men like this to eat from my hand. If only Brayden could see me now. Stupid fucker lost his chance long ago.

When we stepped out of the bar, the chilly air whipped around me and I immediately missed my panties. We reached the curb to call a cab—or so I thought. Instead, I was pleasantly surprised when a black sedan pulled up in front of us. Jackson opened the rear door so I could get in. Once I got inside the posh interior of the car, he closed the door and got in on the other side.

"Going home, sir?" asked the older gentleman driving the car. He had an English accent that was quite adorable.

"Yes, George," Jackson affirmed smoothly. Reaching over, he rested his hand on my upper thigh. Sitting in the car made my dress inch up. Considering the location of his hand and my lack of panties, I could feel the heat from his pinky finger just centimeters from where I truly wanted it.

"So, do you play this game often?" he inquired.

"Every weekend," I told him saucily. His pinky finger softly stroked back and forth causing me to shift a little closer to him, needing to be touched.

"How does a beautiful woman, like yourself, get herself involved in such an unusual game?" he asked, sounding like he genuinely wanted to know.

Annoyed at his question, I sighed and changed the subject. "So, what do you do for a living?"

He sat quietly, realizing I didn't want to answer his question before he finally muttered, "I'm a businessman." *Vaguest answer ever.*

For the rest of the short ride to his place, we sat in silence. His pinky still stroked my thigh, but I was in another place mentally. *Why do I play this game?* Oh, that's right—fucking Brayden. The man had changed me that night but I could honestly say I felt fine. I wasn't heartbroken anymore and I was having fun. Why, then, did I get the feeling that I was being judged by Jackson? *Asshole better make it up to me.* There was no way I was letting him ruin my weekend fun with his judgmental undertones.

The car finally came to rest in front of a posh-looking building. Jackson got out, opened my door for me, and lent his hand to pull me out of the car. I was pretty sure he just got a sneak preview when his eyes darted between my legs momentarily.

Once out of the car, I admired the building. It had recently been renovated. And even though it boasted of newer colors and detail, it still had the charm of all the older buildings in this city. I'd never tire of appreciating these structures. Wishing I had my camera, I vowed to remember to come back and photograph it.

"Come on, let's get inside. The wind is picking up and some of us aren't dressed properly for it," he smirked. He placed his hand on my lower back and guided me inside.

If I thought the outside was pretty, the lobby was absolutely stunning. It had high ceilings and gold detail. The furniture and fixtures were quite ornate. He led me to some elevators, punched in a code on the keypad, and then pushed the "P" for penthouse. Jackson lived quite well, it would seem.

After we silently rode to the top, the doors opened to a sleek, modern-looking loft. Greys and blacks seemed to be the color scheme.

"Andi, can I offer you some wine?" Jackson asked me as I sat my purse down on the entryway table. When I nodded, he whisked away to the bar area just off the living room. "So it's safe to presume that personal inquiries are off subject in our little game?" he asked as he poured two glasses of red wine.

"You presume correctly, Jackson. I feel like we can have some fun but please, let's just make it about sex. I am not really into spilling details about my life," I said to him. "It's not even worth the breath quite honestly."

He studied me for a moment, trying to understand my answer. Finally walking back over to me, he handed me my wine, and I greedily drank it down. He just raised an eyebrow and handed me the other glass so he could go back and refill the now empty one.

Things had been completely awkward since the moment he questioned my motives for my game in the car. Pepper would probably like that about him. Damn him. Damn her. The earlier spark seemed to have fizzled, and I was at a loss as to how to get it back.

Taking matters into my own hand, I sucked down the second glass and glided over to him. Once we were touching chest to chest, I wrapped my arms around his neck and tilted my head up, inviting him in for a kiss. He set the glass down on the table beside him and leaned down until his lips were almost touching mine. I licked my lips to draw him in further, and he took the bait, claiming my mouth furiously. The spark that had dwindled roared to life as we tasted each other. He nibbled at my lip and sucked on my tongue, causing me to moan into his mouth. My hands made their way to his perfect hair and I took pleasure in pulling it and messing it up for him.

His hands made their way to my ass and he roughly grabbed it, pulling me closer to him. I could feel how excited he was, now that I was pressed firmly against him. His hands suddenly slipped under my dress and yanked it up over my hips. As he continued to kiss me, one hand slipped to my sex and began rubbing me. I shivered at the touch and moaned again into his mouth, causing him to growl.

"I need to see you naked," he said gruffly, pulling away.

"Lead the way, hot stuff," I purred back at him.

He surprised me by scooping me up into his arms. When I squealed, he laughed and stalked into his bedroom with me in tow. Unceremoniously, he dropped me onto his gigantic bed.

"Hey! Asshole!" I giggled. He squatted down before me and pulled off my shoes. Taking both of my hands, he pulled me up off the bed to face him. Reaching behind me, he unzipped the zipper to my dress and it fell to my hips revealing my breasts that were carefully tucked away in my man-killer bra. He licked his lips appreciatively and continued to undress me by easing the dress the rest of the way off of me. Helping him out, I unclasped my bra, finally freeing my breasts. He slid my bra down my arms and tossed it aside.

"Wow, you are an absolutely gorgeous woman."

Smiling, I taunted, "Don't be a tease. Show me what's under the suit, Jackson." When he didn't make any moves to undress, I unbuttoned his jacket, pushing it off his shoulders so that it dropped to the floor. Following the jacket, I started unbuttoning his dress shirt and loosening his tie. He finally decided to assist and removed the tie. Once the last button had been undone, he ripped his shirt away, revealing a very sculpted, tan chest.

Instinctively, I ran my hands up his abs and over his pecks. He had a perfect body. Slipping my hands downward, I unbuckled his belt for him and then unfastened his pants. He pulled down the zipper and the pants fell to his ankles, leaving me to admire his physique in just his black boxer briefs. Keeping his eyes trained on mine, he removed the boxer briefs and his hard length bounced out.

Jackson had an amazing body, and I was ready to play. He sensed my desire and gently pushed me backwards onto the bed. Kneeling down, he grabbed my hips and yanked them to the edge of the bed. I started trembling just thinking about what he was about to do. Pulling my legs over his shoulders, he bent over and placed a soft kiss on my clit. He then slipped out his tongue and dragged it between my folds, causing me to buck off of the bed. Grabbing my hips again, he pressed them into the bed, keeping me in place.

He quickly began an insane pattern of licking, sucking, and nibbling. I started hissing air as my orgasm neared. Needing to touch something, I threaded one hand in his hair and used the other to tweak my nipple. When he thrust two fingers into me, I shuddered with delight as my orgasm came crashing down over me. "Jackson!" I shouted, pulling at his hair as my body clenched around his fingers, milking the last of my high.

Jerking himself away from me, he walked over to the bedside table and retrieved a condom giving me a great view of his nice, round ass. He ripped open the package and slipped it over his gigantic cock. Pushing me farther up the bed, he settled himself between my legs and bowed his head to kiss me gently on the lips. Grabbing his head with both hands, I tugged him to my mouth and deepened our kiss by slipping my tongue inside.

We kissed hard for a few minutes until we were both panting for air. I could feel him lining up his tip with my entrance, teasing me. "Jackson, I need you," I begged, nudging my hips upward. Giving in, he pushed himself inside, causing us both to moan simultaneously.

He began thrusting into me, quickly making my orgasm sneak back up on me. The slapping of our bodies made a beautiful sound as we both neared the edge of coming.

"Jackson, I'm going to come again!" I shouted as he continued to pound into me. Just as internal fire overcame me, signaling the start of my orgasm, he groaned and slowed his thrusting. My aftershocks clenched around his cock making us to flinch with each one.

When it finally stopped, he chuckled. "Woman, you are so fucking sexy. We just finished and I'm counting down until we can do it again. You are amazing," he praised. *Yes, this I know, thank you very much, but thank you for the ego boost.*

"Thanks. You aren't so bad yourself," I joked, grinning at him.

Pulling off of me, he strode into the bathroom to dispose of the condom. I jumped up and started redressing, realizing it was getting late. Earlier, I had promised Olive that we'd go grocery shopping together tomorrow. She hated to go by herself. Considering she had stayed home tonight, I'd need to get some sleep if I had any hope of getting up at the crack of dawn with Olive.

When he came back out of the bathroom and saw me dressed,

he frowned.

"Jackson, I need to leave but we can certainly meet up again tomorrow. It's been fun," I assured him, smiling.

"Andi, it's late. Please, stay here tonight," he said, the frown still on his face.

"Jackson, I only live about ten minutes from here. It'll be fine. Here, let me see your phone. I'll text myself so you'll have it and we can set something up for tomorrow," I protested, sighing because he was starting to be a tad difficult.

"Fine, but George is taking you home. You are not taking a cab at this time of night alone," he bellowed, eyes challenging mine. I rolled my eyes, conceding. He let out a breath and called George. "George, I'll need you here to take Andi home. I don't want her taking a cab. Yes, fifteen minutes is fine," he agreed and hung up. Reaching over, I snatched his phone out of his hand and started texting myself.

Unknown Number: Hey sexy. I can't wait to have some more good times with you. How about I take you to a fabulous restaurant? You like sushi? You look like a sushi and sake kind of girl. I bet you like flowers too. I'll make sure to bring you some. ;)

I handed the phone back to him, laughing. Suddenly my phone chimed in the other room. I slipped my feet into my shoes and hurried to my clutch in the entryway. A few moments later, after he'd thrown on some pants, he followed me in there.

"Some guy just texted me and wants to take me on a date," I teased, winking at him.

"Well, are you going to accept his offer?" he asked, chuckling at my silliness.

"I'll think about it. Maybe he can text me tomorrow afternoon and confirm," I suggested as I walked to him. I stood on my toes and kissed him chastely before turning to walk away. Right before

I got more than a couple of feet away, he grabbed my wrist and pulled me back to him.

"See you tomorrow," he promised and pulled me in for a passionate kiss. I tried stepping away but he sucked my lip between his teeth and gently bit. Giggling, I reached under his arms and tickled his bare ribs to get him to turn me loose.

Loud, boyish laughter resonated in the room as he squirmed away from my fingers. Ah ha! Big, powerful Jackson was ticklish. I loved it.

"You're ticklish! Oh, this is going to be fun!" I told him, smiling evilly. He had a huge smile on his face and both hands in a surrender position, backing away from me.

"Woman, you tickle me again and you are getting stood up for your date tomorrow," he threatened, still grinning.

Walking out the door, I shouted back at him, "See you tomorrow, Jackson." Big, serious Jackson was sexy. But ticklish, boyish Jackson was pretty adorable too.

A DARK TWO WEEKS...

It's been a fucking week. I don't feel better—I feel fucking worse. Fuck. Fuck. Fuck. Fuck Brayden. Fuck Pepper and her annoying prods to get me to eat. Fuck my teacher's emails inquiring on my whereabouts. Fuck everyone.

The slamming door lets me know Fucking Pepper is back. Fuck her. "Dammit, Andi. Get your ass out of that bed!" she shouts, ripping the covers off of me.

"Fuck you, Pepper!" I scream back at her, tears filling my eyes again.

"Fuck yourself, Andi. You're going to a doctor. Get up. Now! You are depressed and you need some help," she rants, grabbing my wrists and yanking my frail body from the bed.

We struggle but she ultimately wins because she's Fucking Pepper. She snatches up some jeans and throws them at me. Today I am going to get fucking help. Fuck that.

Chapter FOUR

"Wake up, lazy! I already let you sleep half the day away. I'm ready to go to the market. We're completely out of everything," Olive chirped, bouncing on the bed next to me.

Groaning, I tossed my pillow at her. "What time is it?" I asked, too tired to even look for myself.

"Sweetie, it's ten-o' clock. We're wasting daylight. If we don't get going soon, the market will be packed," she whined. I was powerless against Olive's cute pleas.

"Ugh, fine! But I am taking a shower first," I replied as I dragged myself out of bed.

My head was still pounding from the drinks I had last night. I'd had fun with Jackson but had been ready to leave after our second round. There was no way I was going to spend the night with him. That totally would go against my rules.

After I'd showered and thrown my hair into a wet bun Pepper would approve of, I put on a pair of jeans and a hoodie. No makeup for me this morning. Olive was perched on the arm of the couch, waiting for me when I finally made it in the living room a half hour later.

"All right, hon, I'm ready, but let's stop by Jeanie's on the way. I need a bagel and some coffee," I grumbled as I picked up my purse.

"Definitely!" she agreed, her face lighting up. Olive loved Jeanie's because that's where we'd found each other.

After a twenty-minute walk mostly of us rehashing our evenings, we finally arrived at Jeanie's. Jeanie waved at us when we walked in.

"Couldn't stay away, huh, Miss Andi?" Jeanie questioned, shaking her head. I might not work there anymore, but it would remain one of my favorite places.

"Of course not, Jeanie. I already miss you!" I beamed. She waved me off, gruffly turning to get our order going. There was no sense in trying to tell her you'd try something different. Jeanie just gave us what she felt like making. Olive and I found a table by the window and sat down.

"So are you seeing him again tonight?" Olive asked, continuing our conversation.

Grinning, I told her, "I'm pretty sure we'll go out again. I showed him a good time." She giggled at my insinuation. Pepper got annoyed but I could always count on Olive to want to live vicariously through me. Pepper said that eggs me on.

Jeanie walked up and set down two coffees as well as two everything bagels with cream cheese. The woman knew me well. I handed her a twenty but she rolled her eyes and went back to the register. Olive and I ate our breakfast, chatting about her next modeling gig when the door to the café jingled.

Instinctively looking up, I was surprised to see the bartender from last night and Jackson. Dammit! I looked like a hag this morning.

"He's here!" I hissed to Olive, trying to hide my face. He looked sexy in a pair of low-riding jeans and a fitted Henley. I was about to die of embarrassment from looking so awful compared to

Jackson. *Why did I have to be so lazy this morning?*

Olive stole a glance their way and snickered. "Wow, he is cute. You didn't tell me he had piercings and tattoos!"

"Uh, not him. He's just the bartender. Jackson's the dark-headed god over there in the black shirt. I look terrible. He can't see me like this," I whispered, upset with myself.

As if he could feel us staring, he turned, looking in our direction. His laughter at the bartender stopped when his eyes locked with mine. Gone was Man-Killer Andi and here was embarrassed, blushing Andi. He finally pulled his gaze away and paid Jeanie. I tried to melt into my chair. *I bet he's looking forward to our date now. Not.* I'd forgive him if he pretended I wasn't here.

Luck wasn't on my side though, because Jackson and the bartender made their way to our table.

"Hey, Andi. Can we sit with you ladies? Who's your lovely friend?" Jackson asked, eyes twinkling.

"Uh, sure. Please, have a seat. Guys, this is my friend, Olive," I introduced nervously. Jackson shook her hand, smiling at her. "Nice to meet you, Olive. This is my best friend, Ian Dempsey. He owns the new bar, Dempsey's," he stated, making his own introductions.

Ian took her small hand but instead of shaking it, he brought it to his lips and briefly kissed it. "Nice to meet you, Olive," he winked at her. Normally Olive would be shrinking back from this kind of contact, but she was actually blushing. Black women can definitely blush.

"This is Andi, Ian, but I think you two have already met," Jackson finished.

"Nice to see you again," he replied in his thick Irish accent. I only got a handshake. *Looks like Ian is sweet on Olive, and I think she might actually feel the same.*

Ian launched into talking to Olive, asking her about what she did for a living and commenting on her gorgeous eyes.

Jackson leaned over and whispered into my ear, distracting me from their conversation, "You look so beautiful, Andi."

My cheeks immediately reddened because I felt like he was teasing me, considering I was in no way beautiful at the moment. "Yeah, sure. You just want to make sure you get laid tonight. Don't worry, I'll be pretty before tonight," I grumbled, rolling my eyes.

He grabbed my hand and his hot breath shot into my ear as he said with no humor in his voice, "I don't fucking lie. You are beautiful. You look like an angel sitting in the sunlight by this window. Don't ever downplay your looks."

My heart skipped a few beats. Okay, so maybe he hadn't been messing with me. He smelled of soap and aftershave, which had me swooning.

Jeanie interrupted our moment by setting down the guys' coffees. Everyone turned their attention to Olive as she told several stories from some modeling jobs she had done recently. She was such an innocent, so listening to the things that she described as horrific was really just funny. We were all laughing hysterically at her stories.

Once everyone had finished their coffee, Ian spoke to us. "You ladies should come to the bar tonight. Drinks on me," he suggested, smiling at Olive.

She looked embarrassed, but I saved her from having to tell him no. "Ian, that's sweet, but I actually have a date," I chimed in, winking at Jackson.

The poor guy looked sad. "Well, Olive, you could come. There's going to be a pretty cool band," he piped, in a last-ditch effort to get my adorable friend to see him again.

"I'm sorry, Ian, but I have other plans. But maybe another time?" she asked softly. Poor Olive. There wouldn't be another time. She was letting him down easy. There was no way in hell she would go to a bar. It really was sad because I could tell she felt something for this guy.

"Come on, man. Let's go," Jackson broke in, slapping Ian on

the back as he stood. "Andi, I'll pick you up at seven tonight at your place. Sushi sound good?" he inquired, winking.

"Um, I was thinking steak," I teased. He just grinned as he started walking away. "Wait! I didn't tell you my address," I called after him.

"No worries. George already did," he assured me as he walked out with Ian right behind him.

"Oh my goodness, Andi! Jackson looks like a keeper. Are you sure you want to ditch him after the weekend?"

I rolled my eyes. "Those are the rules, Olive. So, yes, I will be ditching him," I told her honestly. She pouted—actually pouted—at my words.

"Why do you care so much?" I demanded. Looking embarrassed, she glanced down at her napkin and began fiddling with it. "No reason," she whispered quietly.

Suddenly, I realized why she cared. She really had an interest in Ian. "Ah, you like Ian!" I teased.

Her eyes frantically darted to mine. "I do not!" she hissed, but her face told a different story.

"Whatever, chica. I can read you better than you think. No worries. We'll make it happen. I'll make sure you see him again," I promised. Not waiting for her response, I grabbed her hand and pulled her with me so we could head to the market. I had a date to prepare for.

A DARK TWO WEEKS...

So apparently, the doctor says I'm depressed. No shit, Sherlock. It doesn't take a rocket scientist to figure that one out. He said that I need to take antidepressants.

"Did you take your first pill?" Drill Sergeant Pepper asks.

I roll my eyes at her and snatch up the pill bottle. I toss the pill back and chase it with my water bottle. Not wanting to converse, I slide back into the comfort of my bed.

"Look, Andi. I know things are hard for you, but you have to snap out of it. You need to get a hold of that heart and put it in check. Next week you have a finals and you haven't even studied. Please just do it for me. I am dying right along with you seeing you this way," Pepper says with unusual softness.

Sighing, I tell her, "I'll try, Pepper."

Jumping on my bed, she envelops me in her arms and we fall asleep, cuddled like little kids.

Chapter FIVE

The house was quiet while I got ready for my date. Olive and Pepper had gone to dinner at Pepper's parents' house tonight. Her mom needed help getting the house prepped for a fundraiser, so she had told the girls that they could stay the night if it got too late. Turning the music up, I enjoyed my primping time alone. I found a sexy pair of panties and a matching bra to put on. Admiring myself in the mirror, I thought just how much Jackson would enjoy this ensemble.

In the closet, I found a pair of dark skinny jeans and a green tunic. After dressing, I slipped on some heeled boots. I was ready for my date. Definitely in Man-Killer Mode now. Such a far cry from the hideous woman I was earlier today. It was after that moment that I had vowed to never leave the house not made up ever again.

Checking my phone for the time, I realized it was already ten after seven. Well, at least Jackson hadn't arrived yet. Turning off the music, I sat in the recliner, waiting for Jackson to pick me up.

Jerking awake, I realized I had passed out waiting for him. I looked at my phone to check the time and see if he had messaged me. It was 10:15. What the hell? What was worse was that I had no messages from him. Quickly, I fired off a text to him.

Me: Jackson, I think you forgot something. Did something come up?

I got up and went back to my room to freshen my makeup and make sure my hair was still reasonable looking. Fifteen minutes later, I still didn't have any messages from him. *Okay.*

Me: Okay. I'm not sure what to think right now but it sucks. Call me.

I was trying not to seem desperate. There was nothing I hated more than to have a man thinking I was waiting at his beck and call. After I paced the room for another fifteen minutes, a text chimed.

Jackson: Something came up.

What the fuck? Hell no. It was almost 11:00 and I had been completely stood up with a shitty excuse.

Me: I see. Well, have a nice life.

There. I officially ended something that had potential for a lot of fun. Whatever. Grabbing my purse, I headed out the door. I was going to Dempsey's to see the band Ian had mentioned earlier today. Maybe I'd find a new prospect. The weekend was not over yet.

After the quick cab ride over, I hopped out and headed toward the door with my twenty ready in hand. I had catching up to do. Stalking up to the bar and sliding up onto the only vacant seat, I met Ian's shocked stare.

"Andi, I didn't expect to see you here," he stammered, realizing I was supposed to be with Jackson.

"I'll take two shots of Jägermeister and a Corona," I told him, snubbing his statement. I slapped down another twenty.

Ignoring my twenty and my response, he turned to make my drinks. A few minutes later he set them down in front of me. Quickly, I knocked back the two shots and chased them with my beer. When I gave him the look that said I needed another round, he simply nodded and repeated my order. After the second round, I realized I was quickly getting fucked up.

"I'll take another round," I slurred to Ian. He rolled his eyes and made me another round. While I was waiting, some douchebag sidled up next to me. His hair was slicked back and he reeked of cheap cologne.

"I'd like to throw this blond bimbo over the bar and fuck her tight little ass," he suggested in a snarky tone to his equally douchebaggy of a friend, both of them laughing hysterically.

Before I could even formulate a response, Ian slammed his fists onto the bar in front of them and glared their way. He looked quite fearsome with his piercings and angry Irish temper flaring. "Get the fuck out of my bar. We absolutely will not condone any type of derogatory comments to any female in this bar," he growled. The guys started backing away and were met with Meathead grabbing each of them by the neck, leading them out of the bar.

"Thanks, Ian," I acknowledged, turning back to my drinks that were now waiting in front of me.

"You might want to slow down, Andi," he warned as I sucked down two more shots.

I giggled at him and nearly fell off the stool but managed to pull myself upright again.

"He's not a bad guy," he informed me as he wiped down the counter in front of me.

Instantly, my temper flared. "How would I know? He never gave me the opportunity to see. It's cool. It was just sex, Ian. I'm a big girl." I was annoyed that he was trying to defend his friend to me. Me, the girl who had been stood up. "I'll take two more," I ordered as the room spun momentarily.

"I think you've had enough, Andi," he remarked, scowling.

"Dammit, Ian! Give me two more fucking shots and I'll leave. Your dumbass friend stood me up without so much a reason. You at least owe me that just for being his fucking friend," I burst out, getting pissed that he was trying to cut me off.

He sighed heavily and slammed two more shot glasses in front of me, filling them up. Smiling, I tossed those two back as well. The band started up again so I decided I would go dancing. Feeling more and more affected by the shots by the second, I half-danced half-stumbled toward the stage.

As the music thrummed on, I started dancing, running my fingers through my hair. A couple of different guys tried dancing with me, but I was so wasted, that I could barely stand and they lost interest. When the set finally ended, I started jumping up and down, shouting, "Encore!" The world began spinning wildly on me and I completely passed out, slamming my head on the hardwood floor.

When I came to, I was being carried by a pair of strong arms. The arms carried me straight to a black sedan, and I passed out once more.

A DARK TWO WEEKS...

The pills help take the edge off of my insanity. And even though I don't feel like doing anything, I know I have to take my finals. After next week, I'll be able to finally close this horrible chapter on my life.

I have the first of five starting in half an hour. Three are scheduled today and the other two will be for tomorrow. Pepper is watching me from her bed over her book, which means she's analyzing my mood again.

"Ready for your finals?" she asks quietly.

"I guess. Just ready to get them all over with," I say honestly, grabbing up my book bag.

"Good luck, hon," she smiles at me.

Instead of smiling back, I just wave. When I open the door to leave, my heart falls all the way into my stomach. Fucking Bray.

"Andi, hear me out," he pleads, advancing toward me. I'm going to be sick. I'm going to throw up right here. My tears are now falling helplessly down my face. He reaches to wipe them and I jerk away quickly, slapping his hand away.

Pepper realizes something is up and I can hear her bolting to the door. I'm frozen, staring at his handsome face. I hate him. She grabs my hand and pulls me back into the room then rushes out the door, slamming it shut behind her. I can hear them arguing.

"Leave her the fuck alone. Do not ever come back here again. You have left her a fucking mess, and I just made progress with her. You ruined her, Bray. Leave it be and don't ever try to contact her again or I will fucking kill you. Don't test me," Pepper seethes.

Retreating back to my bed, I collapse, trying to tune out his response. God, I hate him. And it hurts so bad.

Chapter SIX

I could feel the sun shining on my face, causing me to squint. Oh my God. I had a splitting headache. *How did I get to bed?* I had really no recollection after falling to the floor last night. Wow, I had made a big fool out of myself last night.

I came to the realization that a heavy arm was draped across my middle. Crap! I took home some stranger last night. I hope to God he remembered to use a condom. Pepper would be pissed at my carelessness.

Finally, I braved opening my eyes and sighed with relief when I recognized the dark, messy hair on the pillow next to me. Somehow Jackson had found me and brought me back to my apartment last night. I remembered now being carried in his muscular arms to his car. My anger from being stood up resurfaced. I pulled my fully clothed body from underneath him and headed to the shower. After I got the bar smell off of me, I would kick him out.

In the middle of washing my hair, the shower curtain flung open and a very naked Jackson stepped in with me. "What the hell,

Jackson?" I shrieked, covering myself. "Get out of my shower!"

"No. Listen, Andi. I'm really sorry about last night. I had a work thing that came out of nowhere and I was caught in the middle of an unfortunate business dealing. I should have made time to call you and explain, but quite honestly, I was too stressed out at the moment," he explained.

Turning my back to him, I said, "Yeah, well, what's done is done. I'm not really into this whole thing we're doing. I think it would be best if you would leave." Instead of getting out like I ordered him to, he grabbed my hips and pulled them to his hardness. I gasped in surprise, but before I could complain, one hand snaked around, grabbing my breast.

The instant his fingers grazed my nipple, I melted into his touch. Damn him. Trying to find some resolve to get him to leave, I started to pull away again, but when the other hand met my clit, I no longer had the willpower to try. He furiously started rubbing my sex, causing me to pant wildly. This wasn't supposed to happen but now I felt powerless against his wishes.

He had me screaming out my orgasm minutes later. Not giving me time to recover, he spun me around and pressed me into the wall with his body. His mouth dipped down to mine and captured it. We began kissing heatedly, not being able to get enough of each other's lips and tongues. Breaking from me, he slipped out of the shower and was back in, dick sheathed in a condom before I could even ask where he went.

Grabbing my ass cheeks, he easily hoisted me up against the wall. Instinctively, I wrapped my legs around him. He groaned at our position and teased my entrance with his cock. "Jackson," I moaned as I threw my head back. Taking it as permission, he slammed into me. Our slippery bodies slapped wildly, and I had to hold on to him for dear life so I wouldn't fall.

He sucked on my neck as he continued to fuck me. My body finally started convulsing as my orgasm coursed through me again. His followed almost immediately after. We both were shaking from the exertion. Pecking my neck, he slowly eased me off of him and back to my feet.

"So fucking amazing," he growled into my ear. I smiled because it had been pretty amazing and unexpected. It looked like I'd let him stay for one more day. The weekend wasn't over yet.

A DARK TWO WEEKS...

Luckily, Pepper was good at being a nagging bitch. Even though I missed the first final, she typed out an email to my professor and got permission for me to take it on Wednesday. Her negotiation skills would make her dad proud.

I walk in with just minutes to spare on my second test. Immediately, the professor hands me the papers and I drop down into a chair to start. The words are just a jumbled mess. I try to focus on the terminology, but it all seems like nonsense to me. Thankfully the test is multiple choice and I can sort of guess my way through it.

After the test, I practically run back to the safety of my dorm. There's a letter on the door. Tearing it open, I can hardly read the words through my tears.

Andi,

I love you. I made a mistake. Please forgive me.

Bray

Fuck you, Bray. You are shredding my heart and I can't take it anymore! Running into the room, I head straight for the bottle of vodka we keep stowed away for emergencies. This constitutes as an emergency. I start chugging until blackness threatens to take over my vision.

Chapter SEVEN

The rest of the shower was quiet and uneventful. I was still pissed at him for standing me up, but it didn't really matter anyway since tonight was our last night together. *Might as well make the best of it.* Opting for comfort, I put on some jeans and a sweater. Deciding he didn't get pretty Andi, I tossed my hair into a wet bun and went with no makeup.

After dressing, I noticed he had put his rumpled suit back on. "Do you have to work today?" I asked him hesitantly. His five-o' clock shadow was really dark now since didn't have anything to shave with in my shower. It looked rugged and sexy as hell.

"Nah, I can take a day off. What do you want to do today?" he asked, pulling me in for an embrace.

"Lunch sounds good since we've already missed breakfast."

Smiling, he agreed, "Okay. I will run home and change and pick you back up in thirty minutes."

I frowned at his words. For some reason, I felt like he might ditch me again. When he saw my face, he dropped his smile.

"Andi, I said I'm fucking sorry. I'm going to come back. We

can grab lunch and then take a walk. I promise I'll be back," he shot out, trying to convince me. I just nodded my response. He huffed and got ready to try and persuade me some more, but the bursting of girly voices through the front door distracted us.

I grabbed his hand and pulled him into the living room with me so I could greet Pepper and Olive.

"Hey, girls! Did you have fun at your parents'?" I asked Pepper.

"Meh, it was fine. Mom was once again her scatter-brained self, and I ended up doing most of it all myself anyway. We got it done though, and the event is going on now as we speak," she told me, glancing behind me at Jackson, clearly waiting for a formal introduction.

"Hey, Jackson," Olive chirped, waving to him.

"Hey, Olive. I'm Jackson by the way," he greeted, extending his hand to Pepper.

She ignored it and spat, "Yeah, you're fucking my friend for the weekend. Wear a raincoat. I don't need her getting any diseases." Jackson slowly lowered his hand, realizing she was just being a bitch. Turning to me, she asked, "So, Andi, how was your date? Olive said sushi was on the menu."

Understanding she was going to be pissed at him, I decided to skirt the issue. "Oh, it was great. You know me, sushi, yum," I lied. Olive just smiled happily, enjoying any sort of details from my date. I sensed Jackson wincing at my words, which made Pepper narrow her eyes at him.

"Sounds fun," she said unenthusiastically, sniffing out my lie.

"Fuck. I stood her up, okay? Then her little ass got wasted at Dempsey's and I had to come rescue her. I was an ass but I'm going to make it up to her today," he huffed out guiltily.

Pepper glared at him. "Oh my God, Andi, I am so glad that today is Sunday. Sometimes your little games suck. I, for one, get exhausted at having to watch you play them," she seethed and stalked to her bedroom, slamming the door behind her.

Looking embarrassed, Olive skittered off to her room, leaving me and Jackson standing awkwardly in the living room. Things were so hot and cold with Jackson. Never a happy medium. Shrugging my shoulders, I walked him to the door.

"See you in thirty minutes, *maybe*," I half-joked as I opened the door. He sighed heavily and pushed me against the doorframe. Leaning forward, he put his lips close to mine as he glared at me with his dark chocolate eyes. They were easy to melt into.

"I will see you in thirty minutes, I promise," he vowed angrily. Then he pressed his lips to mine for a chaste kiss.

Tearing away from me, he ran down the hallway. I guessed he was going to come back after all. Only time would tell.

A DARK TWO WEEKS...

Vodka is good. So good. So, so good! Woah? The room just spun a bit. I better not drink anymore since I have another test today. Okay, just one more shot.

"What the fuck?" demands an angry Pepper as she burst into our room. "Andi! What have you done? You have a freaking test in an hour. Shit!"

"Bray-di-bray-bray-hey," I babble at her before succumbing to uncontrollable laughter.

"Dammit, Andi. Get it the fuck together." She pulls me up to my feet. Geez, the world is swaying again. "We're going to the coffee shop. Let's go," she barks pulling me from the room.

When we start to walk, I stumble a little and almost land on my ass. I hysterically laugh some more. Her glare is menacing at this point.

"He wrote me a letter. He wants me to forgive him," I slur to her as tears start falling.

"Come here, hon. He's a jackass and you're letting him ruin your life. Let's get you some coffee." She sighs and brings me in for a hug.

Chapter EIGHT

Twenty-eight minutes is all he took. Damn, that boy could move. I couldn't help but laugh at him when I opened the door. Chest heaving, face still unshaven, hair waving from air drying—he had actually hustled for me. Okay, today should be fun after all.

"Miss me yet?" he panted, his eyebrow quirking up. Giggling, I swatted at him. He playfully grabbed my wrist and pulled me to him. "Because I sure missed you," he grinned. Gently, he brushed his lips against mine. Adorable Jackson was quite irresistible.

Wrapping my free hand around his neck, I brought him back down for a deeper kiss. Instantly, the chemistry reignited. It was so hot and cold with us, but now it was scorching. I pulled his lip between my teeth and he groaned.

Releasing my wrist, he snaked both of his arms around me to grab handfuls of my ass through my jeans and pulled my body close to his. I pressed my breasts into his chest, needing to feel him there too. As if he realized we weren't going anywhere until certain needs were met, he lifted me up by my hips and my legs automatically wrapped around him. Hastily, he stormed us into my room, kicking the door shut behind us.

Setting me down in front of the bed, he pulled off my sweater in one swift move. He followed mine with revealing his own toned chest. Kneeling, he kissed my lower stomach. I moaned at the touch. Deftly, he unfastened my jeans and rolled them down my legs. I lifted each foot so he could pull them off all the way. His kisses on my stomach continued, and he even placed some along the panty line. Shivering, I ran my fingers through his still damp hair.

He was kissing me all over but not where I wanted him to really kiss me. I leaned into his kisses, hinting at what I needed from him. Finally, he dragged his tongue up the center of my folds through my lacey panties. I cried out in delight. Growling, he pushed me backward until I fell onto the bed. He slid my panties off in one quick swoop.

After he spread my legs, his tongue started lapping me up. I began bucking off of the bed to meet his touch. While he hungrily drove me closer and closer to the edge of sanity, he slid his hands up to my breasts and gently pinched my nipples through the fabric of the bra. The combination of all the sensations caused my body to tighten and shiver as my orgasm pulsed through me.

"Oh my God," I moaned, finally starting to relax afterwards. He chuckled into my sex, his breath tickling me before pulling away.

"You are cute when you come," he observed, still grinning.

"Jackson!" I scolded him while laughing. He looked incredibly sexy standing by the bed with his hair going every direction from air drying with no product. His bare chest had a sheen of sweat across it, making it glisten in the morning sun that streamed in through the window. The jeans he wore hung low on his hips, giving me a glimpse of his Calvin Klein's underneath. Yummy.

Thinking just that, I sat up on the bed and scooted off so that I was standing in front of him. My hands gently ran across his chest and fluttered over his perfect abs. All traces of his playfulness were gone as he gazed intensely down at me, questioning with his eyes what was next.

Pushing just hard enough to get him to walk backwards, I pushed until he was standing in front of the chair in my room. Dragging my hands downward, I found the button to his jeans and unfastened them so that they fell to the floor. I hooked my thumbs in his underwear and jerked them down as well.

"Sit," I ordered. Smirking at my bossiness, he obeyed. Kneeling down, I finished removing the clothes and took a moment to admire his cock. It glistened a bit at the tip, indicating how turned on he was.

Leaning forward, I grabbed it and pulled it into my mouth. He groaned the moment I began tonguing and sucking it. Even though I had slept with many men in the past few months, he was only the second person I had ever done this to. With Bray, I did it because I loved him. With Jackson, I just really wanted to.

His hands laced themselves into my hair as I picked up my pace. I couldn't take his large size very far, but he didn't seem to be complaining.

When I imagined him getting to be really close, I reached up and gently cupped his balls, which sent him over the edge. He spurted hot and furiously into my mouth and I swallowed it down. Once I was sure he was done, I pulled away, wiping my mouth with the back of my hand.

He started laughing. "Need a napkin?" I rolled my eyes at him and got him the only way I knew how—by tickling his ribs.

He jerked up out of the chair and away from me, roaring with laughter. When he laughed like this, it was so infectious. Giggling but determined, I ran after him. He'd only made it to the edge of the bed when I caught him from behind and he yanked away from me again in hysterics. At this point, I was laughing so hard at his aversion to tickling.

This time when I reached for him, he grabbed my wrists and

twisted them around to my back so that we were chest to chest, both of which were still heaving from our laughter. "Woman, you have got to quit doing that!" he admonished.

"What are you going to do about it? It's my secret weapon against you. You have nothing against the all-powerful Andi!" I taunted him.

"Well, it would appear that you are pretty powerless at the moment," he advised. I licked my lips because being unable to move and naked with this really sexy man was freaking hot. His eyes shot down to my lips. The man couldn't stand it when I did that. As if on cue, I felt his cock harden in between us.

Forgetting that we were playing, he ducked his head and began kissing my neck. I started panting heavily as he licked and nibbled. My hips, on their own accord, tried to grind into his. He growled and sucked my neck really hard. "Hey! You'll leave a hickey!" I shrieked, trying to pull away, but since he still had my hands pinned behind me, I was powerless. With one last hard suck, he broke away from my neck and smiled.

"Bastard. I'm going to look like such a slut tomorrow at work," I chastised. His laughter rumbled from his own chest to mine since we were still so close. Giving him a taste of his own medicine, I leaned into his perfect chest, brought his nipple between my teeth, and bit down until he started to release me. But instead of letting me go, he dropped down on the bed, bringing me with him.

He finally let go of my wrists now that I was on top of him on the bed. His hands made their way up to my hair, and he pulled my head to his so he could press his lips to mine. Suddenly all playfulness was gone and I really wanted him inside of me. I captured his mouth with mine and began exploring with my tongue. His tongue met mine with each movement as we kissed in perfect synchronization.

Sliding my legs on either side of him, I straddled him. He grabbed my hip with one hand and used the other to guide his cock into me. "Oh, Jackson," I moaned as I eased all the way down his length, taking him in me entirely.

Stopping momentarily, I realized he didn't have a condom on.

"Jackson," I whispered as he continued trying to guide my hips up and down over him. "You don't have a condom on." He groaned but didn't stop his motions.

"Shhh, baby. I'm clean. Are you on the pill?" he groaned, thrusting himself harder into me. Oh he felt so good.

"I have an internal birth control device," I panted into his mouth as he continued pushing me up and down on him.

"Good because you feel too fucking good for me to stop, Andi," he growled, sucking my lip into his mouth.

My orgasm was building again and I could feel myself getting so close. His hands slid to my rear and grasped onto my cheeks as his thrusts got faster. The shuddering of my orgasm shook through my body and my sex clutched him. Immediately after, I felt his hotness spill into me.

I collapsed onto him, and he brought his hands to my back, where he gently stroked me. It was so nice lying on him like this. Since today was Sunday, our little tryst would end soon, which made me sad. He was watching me with the same sad look. We were both the stubborn types, and I didn't see either of us proposing to extend our game. Sighing, I kissed his chest and pulled off of him, getting to my feet.

Grabbing my robe from the dresser, I slung it on. "You, stay here. You're my sex slave. I'll bring us some food. You'll stay naked if you know what's good for you," I commanded as I walked out the bedroom door, once again enjoying his boyish laughter behind me.

A DARK TWO WEEKS…

I finally made it through my finals, thanks to a very forceful Pepper. I've managed to try to not think about Bray for the last couple of days since he showed up unannounced. We're about to leave to meet Pepper's parents for a celebratory dinner.

"Hon, we're going to the Brass Apple for dinner. You're going to have to put on something a little dressier than your housecoat and fuzzy slippers," Pepper says tossing me a dress from our closet.

Sighing, I drop the housecoat revealing just my panties and bra.

"Shit, Andi! Have you been eating at all? I can see your fucking ribs!" she shrieks, grabbing the skin around my ribcage.

"In case you haven't noticed, I've been a little depressed. Not too hungry these days," I explain, pulling the dress over my head.

Shaking her head, she slips on some heels. Pepper never dresses up except when she's going to see her father. She lives to impress that man and he adores her.

A chime alerts me to a text. Pepper makes a dive for my phone but I snatch it up before she can get to it.

Bray: *Miss you baby. Please talk to me. See you at graduation tomorrow? My parents miss you and really want to see you too. I told them we just took a break. They don't know the details. We don't ever have to tell them and can go back to the way things were.*

The first tear rolls down before I even know what hit me. I miss his parents, and dammit, I miss him too. So much. But what he did was wrong. Can I ever forgive him? Ripping the dress off of my body, I climb back under the covers in just my underwear.

Pepper snatches up her purse and walks toward the door. I hear her say, "I fucking hate Brayden," under her breath. Me too, babe. Me too.

Chapter NINE

After a very late breakfast of cereal in bed, we lay curled up against each other. There wasn't much we could talk about because of our rules to our game. It didn't matter anyway. Tonight was the end of it and then we'd move along on our merry little ways. I was actually really enjoying our cuddle session today. If I wasn't so averse to dating because of how bad Bray had messed me up, I might actually think Jackson and I could be more than just fuck buddies.

My finger lightly traced the curves of his defined chest muscles. We were both quiet in contemplation. He was absentmindedly running his fingers through my hair. With me sidled up next to him, my head on his shoulder and my leg thrown across his him, it felt serene.

I must have drifted off because the sound of a phone dragged me out of my sleepy fog. Jackson and I must have napped the day away because I could see the afternoon sun setting outside of my window. Realizing it was his phone, I shook him. He woke with a jolt, hopping up to retrieve his phone from his jeans pocket.

"Hello. Hey, man. Yeah, okay. I won't forget," he yawned as he spoke to the person on the other line. "Dude! I said I wouldn't forget. I'll be there."

He tossed his phone on the floor and crawled back into bed, this time settling over me. Leaning forward, he captured my mouth in one of his sensual kisses that I couldn't seem to refuse. Melting to his touch, I immediately wanted more. He moved his lips away from mine and down to my neck. When he started sucking and licking, my legs instinctively wrapped around him. I thrust my hips upward, letting him know how much I wanted him.

Groaning at my movements, Jackson used his hand to tease his cock at my entrance. "Please," I begged him. My body was already wet for him and we were both still naked from before. Without any pleading needed, he rammed into me.

He stretched and filled me just like every time. Moaning, I arched my back as my body was already reaching my peak. As he pumped away, he teased, kissed, and nibbled my tongue and lips. My nails scratched his back as I got closer to coming.

Once again, his mouth found my neck and he sucked hard, marking me. Instead of arguing, the sensation caused me to finally orgasm. Clenching around him in aftershocks, I rode out the rest of mine until I felt his own hot seed gush into me.

Inhaling deeply, he breathed in the smell of my neck just near my hairline. It was so very caveman. I ran my hands up his back to his hair, causing him to snuggle into my bare chest. This closeness with another person like this was something I would always miss and strive to achieve in the most non-threatening-to-my-psyche way. In my case, it meant a weekend of fun, sexy times with someone new each time. And even though it feels different with Jackson, I won't allow myself to go there. I had made a promise to myself that I didn't intend on breaking.

"Who was on the phone?" I asked out of curiosity.

"My brother. He has the oldest child syndrome. Thinks he can tell me what to do. I can still kick his ass. Once I turned fifteen, he learned real quick," he chuckled, the vibrations rumbling into my chest. His voice held such fondness while he spoke of his brother.

"You guys sound like you have a close relationship. I have a sister but we're not close at all. In fact, my family and I have never been close. That's one reason why I click with Pepper so well. She's the sister I wish I had and her parents treat me as one of their own." We were quiet as I thought about how I'd only spoken to my family a few times just this year.

Breaking me out of my thoughts, Jackson asked, "Are you hungry? We should probably eat soon." I sighed because I really didn't want to lose any more time with him. Monday was sneaking up on me awfully quickly.

"Let's order pizza. We can eat here," I told him as I wiggled underneath him, indicating I needed to get up. His hot breath tickled my nipple before he pulled it into his mouth. He sucked and nibbled at it until I was wet and pulsing for him again. This man drove my body insane with need.

I felt him harden, pressed against me. It looked like I had similar effects on his body too. In one swift moment, he flipped us over so I was now above him. Catching his drift, I straddled myself over him, allowing him to guide his cock into me. As I began riding him furiously and my tits bounced, I couldn't help be saddened by the thought of not getting to do this after this weekend. Bummer. C'est la vie. That's life.

A DARK TWO WEEKS...

I successfully avoided Bray during graduation but as we are leaving, his mom Connie's voice brings me to a complete halt. "Sweetie! There you are!"

I cringe but sigh in relief once I notice she isn't with Bray. "Hi Connie," I say meekly as she envelops me in a hug that intoxicates me with smells of family and warmth.

"Honey, we've missed you so much. And Brayden is absolutely heartbroken over your breakup." My chin starts to quiver when I think about the fact that he isn't the only one I lost throughout this whole ordeal. "I know he said you needed time to think about things, but, Andi, he's miserable without you. Surely you two can work things out. And, honey, you're a bag of bones. You haven't been eating!"

Biting my lip to keep from losing my composure, I blink back my tears before trying to speak. "It will take some time for me to get past some things, Connie. I don't know that we can ever get back to where we were," I honestly say to her. She frowns at my words but her eyes light up as someone approaches me from behind.

My entire body tenses when I hear Bray whisper, "Andi." I have to escape. There is no way I can be here with him right now. Trying to ignore him, I start walking away, but he grabs my frail wrist, halting me. "Andi, please hear me out," he pleads sadly. His grip is firm so that I can't pull away. He draws me to him so that we are facing, and I inhale his familiar scent. My tears fall shamelessly down my face.

He tightens his arms around me in a strong embrace and I start sobbing uncontrollably. "Jesus, Andi, you're thin as a rail. Have you not been eating?" Shaking my head against his chest, I allow him to hold me for a moment. He has hurt me so badly, but his touch is a salve to the constant burn in my heart.

He kisses me on top of my head and I try hard to just live in this moment right now. I am completely comforted as his hands rub circles on my back. Can we work this out?

As if he's reading my thoughts, he whispers into my hair, "We can work this out, babe. I love you. I fucking messed up but I'll prove to you that we can fix it." I want so badly to believe him.

He brings his hand to my cheeks, moving me away so he can look into my teary eyes. He's so damn beautiful. Without any further words, his lips meet mine and I'm instantly soothed by his familiar kiss. The kiss is sweet and promising. I miss him so fucking bad. We can do this. I can forgive him.

When we finally pull away and step apart, I admire him in his graduation gown. My hope turns to horror when I see two hands belonging to none other than the bitch with big tits snake around his waist. "Hey there, babe. I've been looking for you," she says sweetly.

My breath catches in my throat. I hear Connie gasp nearby. Bray's eyes dart nervously to my eyes before turning angry as he twirls around to face Big Tits. "What the fuck, Steph!" he growls. The world blurs around me as reality slams back into me. A familiar feminine hand grasps mine and quickly pulls me away from the unfolding situation. Pepper is always there when I need her most. I let her drag me away from him for good.

Chapter TEN

After we'd dressed and pigged out on pizza, Jackson and I curled up on the sofa together. Pepper and Olive had gone to dinner earlier, thankfully giving us some privacy. It was clear that Pepper had issues with Jackson and was just biding her time until the weekend was over.

Flipping absentmindedly through the channels, I thought about how unhappy I was that the weekend was almost over. I felt cheated a day because of yesterday. Jackson stroked my hair as we cuddled in comfortable silence.

Tomorrow I would start my first day at Compton Enterprises. Considering I'd been job hunting for five months after graduating, I was completely thrilled about finally finding something. I'd bought a few new suits that said "I'm classy but still cute." With everything I had gone through after the breakup with Bray, I felt that things were about to look up.

I must have dozed off because I was jostled awake as I felt Jackson carrying me to my bed. "Let's take a shower," I told him groggily. He set me down by the bed and pulled off his t-shirt and jeans, heading to the shower. I followed suit with my own clothes. The steam was already filling the bathroom by the time I made it in there.

When I stepped into the shower with him, he gave me a smoldering look. Pouring some body wash into the loofa, he began washing my body. Once finished, I took it from him and cleaned his body as well. He pulled me closer until our fronts touched. Ignoring his hardness, he washed my hair very gently like he was cherishing this moment. I closed my eyes and allowed myself to enjoy his touch. Once he finally finished, I did the same for him, and he groaned as I scrubbed his scalp with my fingertips.

Turning off the water after we had rinsed off, he reached out of the shower, grabbing two towels for us. He wrapped his towel around his waist and used mine to dry me off. His movements were slow and deliberate, so by the time he finished, I wanted him badly.

He used a finger to lift my chin so that I was looking at him. His eyes were so expressive as they searched my own, asking me silent questions. Feeling raw and exposed, I leaned forward and gently kissed his lips just to avoid his gaze. He deepened the kiss as he explored my mouth with his tongue.

Every time we'd had sex so far, it was just hot fucking. This time, I felt, would be different. It was a goodbye to what might have been. He pulled his lips away and continued his kissing on my neck. My body shivered from wanting to make love to him. I just couldn't seem to get my fill—no pun intended.

His lips carried themselves farther down until he had my nipple in his mouth. I moaned as his tongue ran across my sensitive flesh. "I'm going to fucking miss this," he spoke softly between kisses.

"Me too, Jackson. Me too."

K. WEBSTER

The banging on my bedroom door jolted me awake. "Andi, get up! You're going to be late!" Pepper yelled from the other side. Throwing Jackson's arm off me, I jumped from the bed to look at the clock. Shit! I had to be there in forty minutes.

Running to my closet, I grabbed some panties and a bra from my dresser along the way. Frantically, I slipped them on and started fussing over my suit. Once I finally got it on, I chose a pair of thigh-highs and quickly slipped them on.

Deciding a sleek bun would be the way to go, I was able to style it in a way that seemed professional. Since time was running out, I applied a minimal amount of makeup, brushed my teeth, and spritzed on some perfume. Making my way back to my closet, I stepped into a nice pair of heels. Before heading out, I slipped on some pearls and matching earrings.

Striding back into the bedroom, I almost didn't want to wake him. He looked absolutely gorgeous lying on the bed with a blanket barely covering his naked ass. If only I could figure out a way to keep him locked away in my room forever.

After a sad sigh, I walked over and shook him awake. "Jackson, you have to get up! I'm going to be late for my new job and you need to leave. I've had a lot of fun with you but the game is over and it's time for you to go," I ordered as he groaned sleepily. "Jackson. Seriously. Get up. I have to get across town and I've only got 20 minutes."

He rolled out of bed, leaving the sheet behind, giving me a nice view of his perfect body. "The game's over, isn't it?" he asked sleepily.

"Yes, Jackson. It's over and I have to get to work. I'm sorry. I wish we had time for breakfast or even coffee for that matter but I really need to go."

Jackson grabbed my face with both hands and kissed me quickly. "Surely you have time for a quickie. Just one more time, babe," he pled, walking me backwards until my bottom hit the dresser, stopping me. He grabbed my hips and set me on top of it. I

62

shook my head no but he stopped me with a deeper kiss this time and slipped his hand under my skirt. Oh God. I so didn't have time for this.

His finger connected with my clit through my panties and I instantly melted to him. "Jackson, fuck me quickly," I moaned. He continued his motion with his finger until I could feel myself beginning to come apart from his touch. "Oh God, I'm going to come!" I shouted to him. When my orgasm was almost about to shudder through my body, he pulled away his finger, causing me to cry out.

Shoving my skirt up over my hips, he hooked my panties with his thumbs and jerked them down off of my feet. I spread my legs for him when he pulled me to the edge of the dresser to gain better access. Jackson got right to business as he shoved his cock into me. I screamed in pleasure and wrapped my legs around him. My heels were digging into his back, and I considered kicking them off but I wanted to mark him a bit so he'd have something to remember me by.

My orgasm jolted through me without warning and I shuddered around him. I grabbed both hands full of his hair and rode it out until I felt his own release inside of me.

Our eyes met each other as we realized that this was goodbye. He leaned forward until our foreheads touched and pinned me with his stare. We stayed there for a delayed moment before I quickly kissed his lips and gently pushed him away from me. Sighing, he stooped down and picked up my panties, sliding them back up my legs and over my hips.

He pulled me off of the dresser to my feet and jerkily yanked down my skirt, putting it back in place. Turning quickly, he strode over to his clothes and threw them on. He grabbed my hand as I picked up my purse and we headed downstairs so I could hail a cab.

Luck was on my side because a cab quickly pulled up. Jackson grabbed me one last time and kissed me passionately. My eyes were teary as I told him goodbye and ducked into the cab. He watched me intensely as I drove away. Damn, I would miss that man.

A DARK TWO WEEKS…

Pepper helps me crawl into bed, frowning the entire time. She looks hesitant to leave me but I know her family is waiting to have a celebratory dinner with her. With a pat on my back, she leaves wordlessly.

Bray allowed me to get my hopes up but then crushed them all over again in an instant. This hole in my heart will never go away. I need my pills to help me feel better. Dragging myself out of bed, I open the cabinet and pull out the vodka. On the way back to bed, I strip down to just my panties and get under the covers.

I pop a pill and chase it with a swig of vodka. The warm burn slides slowly down my throat and instantly distracts me. I take a few more sips of the vodka, enjoying the burning sensation. God, my heart fucking hurts. Dammit, this pill isn't working fast enough! One more pill should be fine. I toss it back and chase it with another long pull of the vodka.

Numbness is finally starting to trickle over my body. Yes, this feels good. Those pills work. One more ought to do the trick. My vision blurs as I try to pull another pill from the bottle. Too difficult this way. I tilt my head back and let some of the pills spill into my mouth. It's like candy! I crunch down but instantly gag on the bitterness and swallow down more vodka to chase away the taste.

I can't feel my tongue or nose or feet. Well hell, there's only couple pills left. Might as well finish off the bottle. I tilt my head back once more and allow the rest to fall into my mouth, this time opting not to chew them.

My body starts to shiver and I realize I'm freezing. I'm freezing yet I'm sweating all over. I'm so confused. The room is spinning wildly. I think I might be sick. Lying down, I fumble for my phone on the nightstand. Better tell Pepper to refill my prescription since I took them all. Wait, shit. That's bad. Isn't it?

Me: Pepakse, oops pils al gon

After hitting send on the text, I call Brayden. I feel darkness creeping in around me and I fear I've done something bad with the pills. I just want to hear his voice one more time.

"Andi, I am so sorry—" he begins when he answers but I cut him off.

"Braaaay, I messssed up baaad," I slur. "Pills go buh bye."

I must have blacked out because I come to just as Bray bursts into my bedroom door.

"Oh my God, baby! What have you done?! No, no, no!" he cries out, pulling me into his arms. "Fuck! You're blue and so cold!" He tilts back my head and shoves his fingers down my throat. Immediately I start vomiting all over his white t-shirt and my bare breasts. Blackness eats away at the corners of my vision again and my world spins out of control.

His fingers are back in my throat again, forcing my gut to wrench once more. The ringing of my cell phone is endless. Brayden is crying hysterically, telling me to "hold on!" but I just feel ready to let go. And I do just that as the darkness sweeps over me once again.

Chapter ELEVEN

Grabbing my purse, I bolted from the cab, telling him to keep the change. It was five after eight and I still had to get to the 57th floor. Jackson and I shouldn't have had that quickie, but it was so worth it. I just prayed that nobody would notice I was late.

Pressing the button to the 57th floor once inside the elevator, I took a moment to breathe and collect myself. I was finally a woman with a job in her field of study. The world of architecture was so fascinating to me and I really missed it. The café didn't hold a candle to the satisfaction I would have doing what I love.

When the door opened, I quickly glanced at my reflection in the mirror. Deciding that I looked presentable, I held my head high and walked up to the front desk. The receptionist looked about ten years older than me and had a nametag that read "Margie" on it.

"Hi there, Margie. I'm Andi, er, Miranda Dalton, here for my first day," I informed her, still breathing a little heavily from this morning's events.

She looked up and smiled. "You're late," she admonished, winking. My own smile faltered as panic set in. "Honey, I'm teasing. Mr. Compton was on a call this morning, so he's not even ready for you yet anyway. You looked like you were about to throw up," she giggled.

Realizing she was a fun person, I smiled back at her. "Sorry, it was a hectic morning with traffic and all. I'll have to make sure to allow myself more time in the mornings," I told her honestly.

"No worries, Miss Dalton. Everyone is really laid back here for the most part, especially Jordan. You'll enjoy working for him. It's his brother that's difficult. Be thankful you don't have to work for him," she whispered.

Before she could divulge any more office gossip, Mr. Compton called me from his office. Smiling at Margie, I quickly walked into the office where the voice had come from. Mr. Compton was a nice-looking young man. Even though he was several years older than I was from what I could tell, he still looked too young to own such a successful company.

Looking up from his desk, he smiled at me. He had one of those familiar faces and I couldn't help but return his smile. "Please, Miss Dalton, have a seat," he greeted, gesturing to the chair in front of his desk.

Taking my seat, I sat up straight, waiting for my instructions.

"Today will be just you getting to know the ropes and other employees. I'd hoped my brother, who's my partner, would be sitting in on the meeting, but he's running late. I know originally I said you would be assisting me but I'll actually need you to help us both out. I'm in the middle of a pretty big company issue that will require a lot of my time with my lawyers. That will leave my brother having to run things. We'll need you to take our calls when you can, set up meetings with our clients, and make appearances at some events. We have people to actually handle busy work, but as our assistant, you'll learn how to actually interact with the clients more so than the work itself. It's probably one of the most critical aspects of our job that they certainly don't teach you in school." He paused to wait for any input that I might have.

"Okay. That sounds like something I can handle, Mr. Compton," I assured him confidently even though I was nervous from Margie's warning about his brother.

"Please, Miss Dalton, call me Jordan. We're informal here. My dad was Mr. Compton. You'll make me feel old if you keep calling me that," he winked at me. "Anyway, we set up a desk between our two offices out front. I'll have Margie show you how to work your phone. We already gave you access to both my and my brother's calendars and emails so that you can help us manage our appointments. In an hour, I'll be out for a meeting but I'm sure you'll figure things out easily enough. Oh, and tomorrow, a junior architect will be joining the firm. Since I've been pulled into more of the handling of the company, we've needed some more help in that area. He won't have much activity in the beginning so I want you to assist him as well. Once he gets a lot busier, we'll get him his own assistant. And remember, you do this job well, there could be a junior architect position waiting for you as well. We like to promote from within whenever possible. That's what happened to my last assistant." He stopped talking and looked behind me.

"Miranda Dalton, please meet my brother and co-owner of the firm, Jackson Compton," he introduced, gesturing to the door. My body tensed up at the name and I whipped around to see the face of *my weekend Jackson*. Shit!

When his eyes met mine, we both mirrored shocked looks. He walked over to my chair and extended his hand. His shocked look fell and was replaced by a glare. I shakily took his hand and shook it, squirming under his fierce look. "Please, call me Andi," I said breathlessly. I was in some serious trouble.

"Excuse me, I have work to do," he scowled, turning on his heel and stalking out.

"I'm sorry I didn't warn you," Jordan apologized. Turning back to him, I frowned. "He's a bit of an ass. He'll be your biggest challenge working here. He's my brother and I love him, but he can be a bear." He shook his head. I just nodded my own nervously. This seriously sucked. Pepper was going to freak when I told her my luck.

Jordan stood so I did as well. He came around the desk and placed his hand on the small of my back, guiding me out to my desk. With his hand still on my back, I glanced up at Jackson's office. He was glaring at me from his desk, momentarily glancing at Jordan's hand on my back. Quickly standing from his desk, he stalked over to his door and slammed it shut. My first day and I was already wanting to quit. *What have I done?*

A DARK TWO WEEKS...

My life is flashing by in pictures like slides on my phone. A picture of me and Brayden kissing at a game. Pepper and me getting a pedicure for my birthday. Me smiling as a kid with a frowning family in the background. A skinny me accepting my diploma. Brayden down on one knee in Central Park. Me and Jeanie at the café. Me, Connie, and Brayden at Christmas one year.

Am I in a car? I can feel bouncing, which is adding to my nausea. Blinking my eyes open breifly, I can see that I'm in an ambulance. An EMT is fussing over me. What grabs my attention is Bray hovering over me, tears running down his face. His two hands have one of mine and he is kissing it over and over. He keeps begging me to "hold on." Hold on to what?

His shirt is covered in vomit. Is he sick? I try to squeeze his hand to comfort him. When I do, just barely, his red eyes dart to mine. Taking one hand away to stroke my hair, he brings his face close to mine.

"Please, Andi. Don't die on me. I love you. I need you. The way I've hurt you sickens me. You have to believe me that I promise I'll never do it again. Please, just stay alive for me," he cries. I'm so confused. Why would I die?

The darkness creeps up again and I try to fight it because I just want to be here with Bray telling me how much he loves me. My eyes tear up as it closes up on my vision. Please, no! Bray, help me! His panicking eyes are the last thing I see before completely succumbing again to the dark.

Chapter TWELVE

The next hour went without incident as Margie showed me how to use the phone and helped me log into my computer so I could access my email and the guys' calendars. Jackson still hadn't surfaced from his office and Jordan had already left for his meeting. After Margie left me to go back to her reception area, I finally had a moment to myself.

I typed up an email to Pepper's work email address.

Pepper,
This is my work email address. Things are not what I expected at the firm. It would appear that Jackson is one of my bosses. How do I get the luck of these things? Worse thing is, he is acting like he hates me. We seriously went thirty minutes without seeing each other. When I left him, he looked sad, almost like he wanted to chase after me. Then, when he arrived at work today, he looked like he wanted to kill me with the daggers he was shooting at me with his eyes. I don't know what I am going to do. This is all so incredibly awkward.

Your friend who makes bad decisions,
Andi

My stomach was really growling now. It was almost lunchtime, but I wasn't sure what time I should leave to grab some food. The idea of having to ask Jackson made me sick. The ping indicating a new email alerted me to my computer screen.

To the girl who makes the absolute worst decisions,
What the hell?! How in the world does this happen? You need
to go in there and lay down the law, Andi. I am so pissed right
now. If I see that asshole, I'll personally tell him what I think.
Just make it through today and we'll grab dinner afterwards.
We can meet at the café at 6. Hang in there, hon.
The girl who told you so,
Pepper

I responded with my confirmation to dinner and quickly looked up when Jackson's door swung open. Before I could ask him about lunch, he stalked past me and out the front door. So he couldn't even talk to me now. What an asshole!

Ignoring my stomach, I answered some calls and input the appointments on Jordan's and Jackson's calendars. I could smell microwaved meals being heated up by the other employees in the breakroom. My stomach growled again. I was screwed because I hadn't seen any vending machines earlier when I'd taken the tour with Margie.

The front door opened back up about twenty minutes later and Jackson came back in. Not looking at me, he stalked past me with a sack of food back into his office, slamming the door behind him. Feeling a little sorry for myself, I felt a tear slip down my cheek. Realizing I was going to have to talk to him, I shakily stood up and walked over to his door.

When I knocked, he gruffly shouted, "Come in!"

I tried to calm myself as I walked to his desk. He still wouldn't look at me. "Um, Jackson? I was wondering what time I could leave for lunch," I meekly spoke.

My stomach growled loudly and his eyes met mine. They were full of heat and anger but he still didn't say anything. I could feel another stupid tear fall. His gaze softened but his tone was still harsh. "Sit," he commanded.

I sat down, trying to keep my shaking to a minimum. By this point, I was starving, and now I was in a battle of wills with Jackson. This day really sucked.

Pulling out two to-go containers from his sack, he sat one in front of me. I looked down at it, confused. "Eat," he ordered. My eyes darting back to his, I frowned. He was opening his own container, avoiding my gaze. I started to stand, grabbing the box so I could eat in the lunchroom but his voice growled at me, stopping me in my tracks. "I said eat. Here," he barked, glaring at me.

Margie wasn't kidding. He was such an asshole! How had I not seen this over the weekend? This couldn't be the same guy who had tenderly stroked my hair while we watched a movie. It couldn't be the same guy who had laughed like a little boy when I tickled him. This man was cold. I didn't like him at all.

Sitting back in my chair, I opened the box. It was sushi. I couldn't help the grin that broke over my face. He remembered that I love sushi. Scooping up a roll with my chopsticks, I dipped it in my soy sauce and greedily dropped it into my mouth.

Considering I was so hungry and I was eating my favorite food, I moaned in pleasure at the delicious taste of the roll. His eyes flew to mine but dropped to my mouth as I licked my lips. When they made their way back up to mine they were full of need. These were the eyes I was used to seeing.

He cleared his throat and turned his attention back to his food, trying to avoid looking at me again. At least I knew he was having trouble keeping up his asshole premise.

I quickly devoured all of my rolls and stood to go back to my desk. "Come here," he whispered, sounding like he choked on his words a little.

My eyes met his, and I couldn't help wanting to have a repeat performance from this morning. Asshole or not, he was fantastic in bed. Gesturing for me to come closer, I nervously walked around to where he was sitting.

"Come here," he quietly ordered again. He took my hand, pulling me a little closer. I closed my eyes as I leaned forward, wanting to kiss him so badly. He chuckled and stuck something in my hand. I blinked open my eyes, looking at what he had given me. A fucking fortune cookie. He let go of my hand and swiveled in his chair away from me. Grabbing the phone, he started dialing and waved me away. Fucking waved me away.

Completely pissed, I stalked out of his office and tried to refrain from slamming the door. Once I got back at my desk, tears stung my eyes again, but this time they were angry. I opened my cookie and read my fortune.

"Everything will be okay. Don't obsess. Time will prove you right. You must stay where you are."

Damn you, wise fortune cookie. Damn you.

A DARK TWO WEEKS...

My eyes flutter open and I take in my surroundings. I'm in a hospital room. I can feel a tube down my throat and an IV attached to my arm. My head is in such a fog. What happened? I can see people seated in my room, but I'm having trouble focusing on them. Tears begin falling down my cheeks as I start crying, further blurring my vision.

I can hear shuffling of feet and whispers before a small hand grasps one of mine. "Shhh, Andi. Everything's okay. They were able to pump your stomach but a lot of the medicine and alcohol is still in your system. The IV is trying to flush it out for you. You scared us when you stopped breathing, so they are keeping you safe with the breathing tube. Don't try to talk. Just know that we're all here with you," Pepper gently comforts me.

I hear her barely whisper, "You need to leave, motherfucker."

And in an angry whisper that matches her, I hear Bray growl, "Fuck no." His hand envelops my other one. My tears are really falling now and I am sobbing uncontrollably.

"I'll get the nurse," I hear my mother say coldly. My mother? If she is here, this is really bad.

Seconds later, a nurse shuffles in. Bray and Pepper are still stroking my hands and whispering soft, gentle things to me.

"When will the psychiatrist be here?" my mother questions the nurse. The nurse informs her that he is making his rounds and that it will be soon. She also tells her that in the meantime she will give me something to relax. I can feel a cold sensation seeping into my vein and trickling up my arm. Trying to fight the pull it is having on me, I squeeze Pepper's and Bray's hands once before the medication wins and fully drags me under.

Chapter THIRTEEN

The afternoon went by quickly because the phone rang off the hook. I handled the clients with ease and was able to force the confusing thoughts about Jackson from my mind. He stayed in his office the entire time. Jordan had come back a while ago and stormed into his office. His meeting must not have gone well because he had been visibly upset about it.

When the work day was almost over, Jordan emerged from his office, looking very tired and stressed. He walked over to my desk and sat on the edge. "How was your first day, Andi?" he asked. He was smiling at me but it didn't reach his eyes.

"Um, it was great. I think I handled things well. The question is, how was your day?" I wondered genuinely.

Reaching his hand up, he rubbed the stubble along his jawline. "I've had better. How did Jackson treat you? Did he act like an ass?" he questioned, looking into my eyes.

His genuine interest coupled with the horrible way things had evolved today had tears forming in my eyes. I tried to blink them away so my boss wouldn't see how I was letting Jackson affect me.

Anger swept across his face as he gently wiped a tear that had managed to escape down my cheek. Jackson's door opened beside me but I ignored it since he was going to do the same to me anyway. Hopping off the desk, Jordan softly ordered, "Come here." He grabbed my hands and pulled me in for a hug. It appeared that we both needed a hug after our shitty day.

Something slamming on my desk caused me to jerk away from Jordan's embrace. Jackson was glaring at the both of us, eyes darting back and forth. His jaw worked furiously, clenching and unclenching. Jordan tensed up beside me and they had a fucking standoff before Jackson finally spoke. "Real fucking professional, Jordan." Without waiting for a response, he stormed out of the office.

Jordan patted me on the back. "Welcome to the gang," he huffed, sighing as he walked back to his office. "Hope to see you tomorrow."

With that, I snatched up my purse and left. Returning was still up for debate.

"I still can't believe it," Pepper murmurs, shaking her head as she sips her wine. We'd already had dinner at the café and had moved to Dempsey's to have some after-dinner wine. It was a slow night at the bar so we were able to find a quiet booth near the back.

"Yeah, it's pretty awful. I am just hoping it will get better. There aren't many jobs out there, so I'd be a fool to quit, but that doesn't make it any easier. If I didn't have my stupid game, this never would have happened," I whined as I downed the rest of my glass. My game was a joke anyway. It was time to stop what I'd started months ago and start trying to act like a normal human being. The server came over and refilled our glasses.

I heard Ian's booming voice behind the bar, welcoming some guys as they walked in. Following his gaze, I was horrified to see Jordan and Jackson.

"Shit, Pepper. They're here. Jordan and Jackson are here. We should go," I urged, scooting out of the booth. When Jordan saw me, he waved and started walking over to me. Jackson jerked his head in my direction and glared at me.

"Andi! Surprise seeing you here. Let me buy you and your lovely friend here a drink," he smiled when he reached our table. Whatever stress he had been dealing with earlier seemed to have dissipated.

"We were about to leave," Pepper informs Jordan, knowing that I was beyond uncomfortable.

"Nonsense! You can have a drink with us. Jackson! Get your ass over here. Ian! Bring a round of drinks to us. Surprise us," he ordered as he scooted into the booth next to Pepper, causing her to yelp. He looked over at her and grinned.

Normally she *could* be as frosty as they come, but right now her cheeks were blazing as she shakily scooted closer to the wall to get away from him.

Jackson finally made it to our table and reluctantly sat down beside me, as far away as he possibly could while still sitting on the same bench. I sighed and turned my attention back to Jordan. Keeping my hands busy, I rolled my napkin and folded it over and over again. Jordan was smiling at me. Clearly he was the more charismatic of the two.

"Excuse my socially inept brother. He doesn't get out much. I blame it on Mom for babying him so much," he chuckled. Jackson grumbled something under his breath and tried to ignore Jordan.

I looked over at Pepper and she had composed herself again. Frosty Bitch was back. "Andi here was just telling me about her wonderful day at work," she said sarcastically, glancing over in Jackson's direction. I cringed at her words. Jordan didn't seem to notice that they were sarcastic, but Jackson flinched ever so slightly.

"Great! I'm so glad, Andi. I think you'll really like it there. Everyone works hard to make it a successful company," Jordan beamed as he bragged about his employees.

When I started to nervously shred my napkin, Jackson's hand covered mine, taking it from me. I couldn't ignore the heat that ignited between us. Quickly, my eyes found his, which were drinking me in. My heart started racing, but thankfully the intense moment was interrupted when Ian set down two rounds of shots. "It's on me, guys," he said, winking at us and returned back to the bar.

Jordan began telling a funny story about one of his newer clients. We were all laughing at him, but I was having a hard time giving him my entire attention. Jackson was beside me, practically knocking me over with the intense waves rolling off of his body. I'd like to assume they were of desire, but I realized it was probably anger at having to sit with me.

We all started to relax a little more as Ian brought another couple of rounds. When Jackson's knee touched mine and stayed there, I froze. The electricity that pulsed through us was almost visible. Pepper and Jordan were talking about some art exhibit, but I could barely understand their conversation because I was too caught up in this moment with Jackson.

When his hand gingerly rested on my thigh, I shuddered at the intimate touch. I'd wanted all day for him to show some indication of the man from this morning and he had finally thrown me a bone. His hand started gently rubbing my thigh over my skirt. I gasped silently when his hand pushed my skirt up, giving him access to my panties.

Jordan and Pepper were now in a heated discussion about something, but I completely ignored them. Jackson slipped a finger underneath my panties and rubbed across my clit. I jerked but forced myself to stay calm. He began a delicious pattern over my sensitive clit. I choked down my panting and eagerly awaited the orgasm that was very close.

With his other hand, he slid my wine glass in front of me and nodded to it. Shakily, I snatched it up and brought it to my lips. My orgasm hit hard and was intensified when he shoved two fingers inside my wet core making me buck off of the seat a bit. Swallowing down my moans with my wine, I shook with my aftershocks. He pulled his fingers from me and slid my skirt back into place. Oh my God, he was something else.

Sliding from the booth, he said to all of us, "I'm tired. I'll see you all later." Without another glance in my direction, he left the bar. Jackson was so damn hot and cold. But the hot was almost worth the cold.

A DARK TWO WEEKS...

"She's coming back to Indiana with us," my mother informs the psychiatrist, Dr. Sweeney.

"Ma'am, I think we need to let Andi decide what she wants to do," he says gently, looking over at me. It has been a couple of days since the accident and they are ready to release me. Dr. Sweeney wants to see me again on Friday.

"Mom, it's okay. I'm supposed to be moving in with Pepper this weekend. I promise I'll be okay. Dr. Sweeney and I have really been working out some of my problems," I assure her, sighing. My mother isn't a very affectionate, loving woman. It is weird that she even appears to care. Dad and my sister Megan couldn't even find time from their schedule to come see me at the hospital.

She sighs but nods in agreement. Dr. Sweeney scribbles out a new prescription for me and asks me to promise that I not take them with alcohol. I nod sheepishly. The whole thing really was an accident. I wasn't really trying to kill myself, but I almost succeeded, even if by accident. If it weren't for Bray, I shudder to think what could have happened.

Bray has remained on constant vigil by my side throughout this entire hospital stay. Pepper refuses to speak to him anymore and gives him death glares when he's nearby. Yesterday, though, Dr. Sweeney put an end to his visits. He said that part of my recovery revolves around healing myself without Brayden's help. Bray was really torn up about his suggestion but said that he really wants to help me and would honor Dr. Sweeney's wishes. After a gentle kiss to my forehead, he left me, saying that when I was healed from all of the pain he'd caused maybe we could work on a friendship at the very least.

I really don't want Bray out of my life but I fear I'll always be in a fragile state unless I handle my problems without him. This weekend I plan on starting the next phase of my life. I'm ready to start living again. The last two weeks have been an awful blur, and I never want to feel that way again.

Chapter FOURTEEN

This morning I was on top of things despite my pounding head from the shots last night. I found a really sexy suit a little on the shorter side now that I knew who I'd be wearing it to impress. After I slipped on some thigh-highs and then some impossibly high heels, I walked over to my full-length mirror and admired the view.

Jackson would have to be dead to ignore me today. My blonde hair hung in sexy curls down my back, my makeup was a little on the darker side today, and my outfit screamed "Fuck me." In a moment of bravery, I slipped my panties off and kicked them to the side. Knowing that I would be working without panties near Jackson almost had me running for my vibrator in my bedside table. Ignoring the desire coursing through me, I snatched my purse and headed out.

Right before we pulled up to the building, I reapplied my red lipstick and paid the cab driver. Heads turned as I walked into the building, boosting the self-assurance that had been stolen by Jackson yesterday. I held my chin up and confidently rode the elevator up to our floor.

When Margie saw me, her eyes lit up. "Hey gorgeous! You're going to knock them dead today. Jordan and Jackson are already in the conference room with the new junior architect, who is absolutely hot. Jordan said to send you in when you got here," she giggled. I smiled and thanked her. Swinging by my desk, I dropped my purse in my drawer and picked up a note on my keyboard. It was from Jackson.

Lunch again today? Same time, same place?

His scribbled request made me smile. Maybe things wouldn't be so bad. And he was definitely going to have a hard time not paying attention to me today. I was hot and knew it.

I strode into the conference room and smiled at Jordan, who was watching me with wide eyes. Jackson swiveled around and actually grinned as he appreciatively took in my appearance. My smile faded when the third chair turned to see what Jordan and Jackson were looking at.

"Andi? Oh my God. I can't believe this!" Bray exclaimed, jumping from his seat and coming toward me. He pulled me in for an embrace, and my eyes closed when I got a huge lungful of his familiar scent. He rubbed my back, not wanting to let me go until someone cleared his throat behind him.

Quickly pulling away, he turned to see Jackson glaring at us. "You two know each other?" Jackson asked, voice rolling with anger.

Not wanting to make things uncomfortable for Bray, I spoke up. "Uh, yes. We went to college together," I half-lied, avoiding Jackson's fiery gaze. I quickly moved to sit down beside Jordan.

"Great! This is really going to be a great dynamic for our team here. Since you two know each other, things will go so much more smoothly," Jordan beamed warmly, patting my bare thigh and then removing it to neaten his stack of paper in front of him.

I looked up to see Bray and Jackson wearing matching glares, this time directed towards Jordan, who seemed oblivious. The testosterone was thick in the conference room today.

Jordan quickly addressed a few things before excusing everyone. I jumped from my seat and bolted back to my desk. Once I sat down and pretended to be preoccupied with booting up my computer, Jackson stalked past me into his office, slamming the door behind him. Shit. Today was even worse than yesterday!

Now, I had to work with someone who was the ultimate cause of the way I was today. Working with Bray was going to prove to be extremely difficult, especially since the pain in my heart I had eradicated pulsed at the sight of him earlier.

Jordan and Bray walked out together, shaking hands before Jordan went over to his office. Bray sauntered over to my desk and glanced at my legs. Dragging his eyes back to mine, he said, "You look really beautiful, Andi." I muttered a thanks and turned my attention to the computer screen. He stood quietly for a moment before walking over to his office right next to Jackson's.

Pepper needed to know today's events.

Pep,
Guess who works here now? Never in a million years could I have predicted this. Imagine the worst possible scenario and you'll be right. Drinks again tonight? This time at our apartment with Olive?
Your best friend who has no luck at all,
Andi

After I hit send, my inbox chimed immediately with her response.

Fucking Brayden.

Sighing at my luck, I got busy returning phone calls and planning meetings for all three guys. The morning flew by, and I was startled when Jackson came out of his office and left without saying a word to me.

I guess we were back to the cold Jackson I didn't like. He had said that we were having lunch, so I was guessing he had gone to go get it.

Brayden suddenly emerged from his office and walked over to my desk. "Want to grab some lunch and catch up?" he asked, smiling at me. I squirmed under his gaze. Everything about this chance encounter had my nerves on edge.

"Jackson went to get some for me. Maybe tomorrow?" I quipped, biting my lip.

His eyes fell to my lips and he looked almost sad when he glanced back up at me. "Sure, tomorrow," he muttered hoarsely and took off out the door.

An hour later, Bray came back in. Stopping at my desk on the way to his office, he asked if he had any messages. "I emailed them to you. Check your calendar. I set up something on Thursday with a Mr. Higgins," I told him.

Glancing into Jackson's office and then back to me, he asked, "How was lunch?"

"Um, Jackson is supposed to be bringing it back," I offered weakly. Considering it was now a quarter to two, I thought I might have been stood up again. When my stomach growled loudly, I clutched it trying to get it to stop.

He frowned at me. "Shit, Andi, you know you get lightheaded if you don't eat properly. Let's go. We'll run down to the café here in the building and grab you a sandwich."

I stood up, quickly deciding that I needed to eat in order to function for the rest of the afternoon. The room spun and I grabbed the desk trying to gain my bearings. Suddenly, two arms were around my middle trying to ease me back into the chair.

"Andi, sit down," Bray urged quietly. "I'll be right back."

I put my head on the desk and waited for Bray to return. When he finally came back about ten minutes later, I was happy to see him. He had a sandwich in one hand and a soda in the other.

Unscrewing the lid, he handed it over to me. "Here, drink this. It will make you feel better so you can stomach the food. You need to bring some snacks to keep up here. Working at a fast-paced firm like this, there may be times you can't eat and we can't have you fainting. You know how you get," he gently chided.

I nodded my head and sipped down the soda. Finally, I felt okay enough to eat the sandwich. Tearing it open, I ate it quickly. He watched me sadly while I ate. This had to be the most awkward situation ever. When I nervously tried to put the lid back on the bottle, my fumbling hands dropped it at my feet.

Before I could bend over to pick it up, Bray had already knelt down to retrieve it. When he glanced up at me, his eyes skittered up my legs, landing right between them. Heat instantly flooded his face as he looked up at me with a smoldering expression. "Fuck, Andi! You're not wearing any panties!" he hissed, glancing there again.

Embarrassment overcame me as I crossed my legs quickly, ending his peep show.

"Is that so?" a familiar voice asked behind him. Jackson was glaring at Bray, who was still crouched in shock. Bray shot up from the floor and spun to face him.

"She has to eat or she will pass out. If you promise to bring her food, then fucking do it," he growled at Jackson and stormed back to his office.

Jackson looked after him and then jerked his gaze back to me. "Shit. I'm sorry, Andi," he apologized, rubbing both hands across his face. "I was having a really bad morning and I completely forgot."

Shaking my head, I avoided looking in his direction and pretended to be doing something on the computer. "It's no problem. Bray got me a sandwich," I answered softly.

I could hear the grinding of his teeth before he grunted and went into his office, closing the door behind him.

A little while later, Jordan came over. "Andi, I need a favor.

The firm is really needing some good publicity. The museum where your friend Pepper works is having a gala event soon. They've already pinned down their sponsors, but I want Compton Enterprises to be the main sponsor. I don't care how much it costs and how much persuading it takes, but please make it happen," he said and went back to his office.

Well, I could always try. I'd get some drinks in Pepper tonight and beg her. Maybe she'd feel sorry for me and pull some strings. If anyone could make something happen, Pepper could.

When Jackson's door opened, I glanced up at him. His hard glare from earlier was gone and the softer side of him was looking at me. "Can you come in here for a minute?" he asked, motioning towards his office.

I stood up and walked over to him. He allowed me to pass and closed the door behind him.

Grabbing my hand, he pulled me to him. My body melted to his but I was still upset with him. "Andi, I am fucking impossible to be around. When I found you on Friday, I looked forward to a weekend of not being my usual self and enjoying the moment. We had a great time and I loved every minute of it. Now that you work here, I'm having trouble being that man you knew because of the person I really am. I am an unhappy person. But you actually make me happy. You're smart, sexy, and confident. I don't deserve someone like you. My shit for brains can't even remember to honor our dates. Please forgive me. I'm really trying here," he pleads, frowning at me, clearly angry with himself.

His confession warmed my insides. We were both damaged people trying to live normal lives. Maybe we could fumble our way through this after all.

I stood on my toes and gently kissed his lips, letting him know that I was trying to forgive him without words. His hands threaded through my hair and pressed me farther into his lips. I moaned because I wanted him so badly. His tongue slipped into my mouth and stroked my own. Our kiss became more fervent. One of his hands slid to my ass and grabbed it. I dropped my hands down to his belt and started undoing it.

He groaned and reached over to lock his office door. Breaking from our kiss, I finished with his pants and pulled them down. His hands grasped the bottom of my skirt and hiked it up over my hips. "Fuck, Andi, you are so fucking sexy. You didn't wear panties for me and I was a dick to you. I don't deserve you," he growled as he reached down to cup my sex.

"Jackson, please fuck me now," I breathed as he stroked my clit. Reaching around me, he grabbed my ass and lifted me onto the credenza. I spread my legs so he could access me better. He reached down and guided his cock into me.

I threw my head backwards as he began pumping into me. My orgasm teased me as it got closer. When I started to moan loudly, Jackson's hand covered my mouth and kissed my neck. "Shhh, baby, shhh," he crooned into my ear.

My body thrashed uncontrollably as my orgasm crashed into me. His pumping slowed as I felt him come. We probably would have stayed like that, milking the last of our orgasms, but a loud knocking on the door made us jerk apart.

Jackson hastily pulled up his pants and quickly fastened them. "Yes?" he asked gruffly even though he was smiling at me.

"It's me, Bray. Is Andi in there? I need to ask her something about my schedule," he requests through the door. Glancing at my legs as I was pulling down my skirt, Jackson reached over and grabbed some tissue from the box on the credenza.

"We're just finishing up. I'll send her over in just a minute," he called out. He came back over to me and crouched. Wiping my leg with the tissue, he cleaned up the remains from our heated moment. Bringing his lips to the inside of my thigh, he kissed it.

Smiling at me, he stood up and walked back over to his desk, picking up the phone to make a phone call. My cheeks flushed and I hurried out of the office to go see what Bray needed. Jackson was so hot and cold, but that was totally freaking hot.

A DARK TWO WEEKS...

"This will be your room," Pepper says with a smile as she gestures to the bedroom. I love everything about this apartment. It has really high ceilings and open windows. The hardwoods are the original and add charm to the building. Crown molding decorates the top of the walls, looking ornate. This place was absolutely gorgeous. For once in the past two weeks, I am genuinely happy.

"Pepper, I'm so excited. This place is fabulous. I promise I'll pay half the rent once I get a real job. In the meantime, I'll buy our groceries," I assure her.

She just waves me away, grinning. "Andi, no worries. I don't care if you pay me at all. You're my best friend. We're going to have such a blast!"

We hug each other and I bask in the power that rolls off of Pepper. She is my rock and I am blessed to have someone like her in my life.

Chapter FIFTEEN

Slipping out of Jackson's office, I quickly go to Bray's.

He's hunched over, looking at some paperwork when I walk in. Closing the door behind me, I walk over to his desk. When he looked up and saw me, he smiled, gesturing for me to sit.

I sat down and waited for him to speak. "Andi, my appointment with Mr. Higgins is on Thursday, as you know. Do you think you could come with me and take notes? I'm trying to get him to accept our offer versus a competitor's. I think having you there will be a good learning experience for you," he informs me.

I nodded, excited to go into the field and meet with a client. "Sure. I mean, as long as it's okay with Jordan and Jackson. Will you clear it with them first?" I asked.

"I already spoke to Jordan about it. He said that was fine and they'll manage without you." He turned his attention back to his computer. "Well, I need to get back to work," he sighed, dismissing me.

When I stood to leave, he stood as well and walked over to

me.

"Andi, this is so fucking hard working with you. I just want to sprawl you out on my desk and make love to you like old times. It has been incredibly difficult to resist doing what I'd love to do to you today." He stepped really close to me, enveloping me in his scent once again, and grabbed a lock of my hair, twirling it between his fingers. "And the fact that I know you aren't wearing panties makes me want you so fucking bad," he growled, pressing his body against mine so I can feel his erection.

Jerking away, I shakily walked out of the office. He had no right to walk back into my life and try to pick things up again like the worst part of my life had never happened.

I went back to my desk and sulked for the remainder of the afternoon. Bray really complicated my life. I'd finally gotten things somewhat sorted out and here he was again, messing it all up.

"Let me take you home," Jackson stated, coming from his office.

I turned and smiled at him. "Okay, let me grab my purse."

As we got ready to leave, Bray stepped out of his office, closing the door behind him. His eyes darted to mine and darkened when he saw Jackson standing near me.

Storming past us, he grumbled, "Andi. Jackson," and disappeared out the door. Yep, definitely awkward. My phone chimed in my purse, so I pulled it out to see who had texted me.

Pepper: Something came up at work. I'm having to sort through it. Our main sponsor just pulled their place and I am scrambling to find a replacement. Rain check on drinks?

Smiling, I told Jackson to hold on a minute and rushed into Jordan's office. "Pepper just texted me saying that their main sponsor pulled out for the gala. Here's her business card. Call her and set it up. I bet she'll be happy to find a quick replacement," I speculated, handing Jordan the card.

He smiled in satisfaction, grabbing the card from me, and picked up the phone to dial her number. "Pepper, hi...it's me, Jordan Compton," he greeted. I turned on my heels after waving bye to him and met Jackson by the door.

Jackson grabbed my hand in his and we headed to his car. George greeted me with his cute accent when we stepped into the vehicle. "Want to grab dinner?" Jackson asked me. I nodded since Pepper couldn't hang out with me anyway. "George, take us to Santino's Grill."

His hand slid to my thigh and I grinned at him. I was more than happy to be spending time with Hot Jackson. He was making his appearance more and more today rather than Cold Jackson.

"What are you smiling about?" he asked me as his hand rubbed up and down my upper thigh. My body shivered like it always did when he touched me.

"You," I answered simply. His eyes dropped to my lips. Knowing it would get to him, I licked them. The light in his eyes ignited and he pressed against my lips with his own. My core ached for him. Unbuckling my seatbelt, I climbed over him and straddled his lap. He groaned and reached over, pressing a button that dropped a divider between the driver and the backseat.

His hands grabbed the bottom of my skirt while I kissed him wildly and yanked it up. He took a handful of my ass with each hand and I grinded myself into him. Removing his hands, he unbuttoned my blazer, slipping it off. Thankfully the windows to the car were incredibly dark because I was about to give them a show otherwise.

He pulled off my camisole, leaving me in just my bra, but quickly fumbled with that and yanked it off of me too. I helped him slip out of his jacket and began working the buttons on his shirt. Once I got them undone, we both pulled it away from him. I leaned forward, kissing him again, this time our bare chests touching.

Grinding into him some more, he practically tossed me off of him so he could pull his pants down. When he got them down far enough, I straddled him again, easing myself onto him. I started bouncing on his cock, making my tits bob in his face. He grabbed them and started sucking and kissing them all over.

My orgasm came surprisingly fast and I almost stopped riding him to allow it to shudder through me, but his hands grabbed my ass again and helped me bounce until his own burst into me. We relaxed, still joined, and I nuzzled my face into his neck. His hands rubbed up and down along my naked back, making me shiver.

We stayed like this in comfortable, silent bliss until the car stopped. I scrambled to throw my clothes back on and Jackson just smiled at me. "You're so beautiful with your 'just fucked' hair. If we weren't already at the restaurant, I'd fuck you again just to keep up your sexy hairstyle," he smirked at me.

Sticking my tongue out, I finished dressing. "And do that again and we certainly will never leave this car," he growled making me giggle.

Once dressed, we stepped out of the car and the heavenly aroma of authentic Mexican food hit me. I moaned at how good it smelled and Jackson squeezed my ass making me yelp. "When you make that noise, it takes everything in me not to bend you over right now," he said gruffly. I laughed and grabbed his hand hurrying him into the restaurant.

After we made it inside, I was mesmerized by the colorfully painted walls and columns, the garish decorations all over the place, and the delicious smells that filled the air. The hostess seated us by a window and set down some chips and salsa in front of us. Speaking in Spanish, she asked a question. Jackson flawlessly recited something back to her in her language and she hurried away.

"We're having margaritas," he informed me, smiling.

I grinned because you can't have good Mexican food without margaritas. "What's good here?" I asked him trying to read the menu that was all in Spanish.

"The fajitas are amazing. You want to try those?" he questioned, taking my hand in his.

"Sounds great. I'm just happy to be on an actual date with you," I replied happily.

A look of regret passed across his features at my words. "I'm sorry, Andi. I told you I suck at this. I'm trying. I promise."

The server set down two giant margaritas and a bowl of queso. He let go of my hand so we could eat our appetizer. Speaking quickly, he ordered for us, and she once again scurried away.

"So tell me how you know Brayden," he said, turning serious. My eyes jerked to his because I certainly didn't want to have this conversation right now. His eyes darkened because he knew deep down that Bray was more than just a college mate.

Sucking it up, I resolved to tell him the truth. "Bray and I met our first year in college. We were both getting our degrees, majoring in Architecture. He was my world," I confess softly, sipping at my margarita. "We dated for almost four years. Last March, he very romantically proposed to me in Central Park." I sighed because the sad part was coming. Jackson was waiting patiently for me to continue but still had a scowl on his face.

"I was so excited about our wedding. One day I got out of work early and wanted to surprise him. I found him banging some chick. Jackson, it absolutely devastated me," I whispered, tears forming in my eyes. When he jerked out of the booth, I thought he was going to leave me there, but he sat down beside me, scooting me over with his hips.

He draped his arm around me and pulled me close. Blinking back the tears, I continued. "I didn't eat hardly at all for two weeks. He would try and contact me but I ignored him. Pepper also helped take care of keeping him away from me. My depression was so bad, that she convinced me to see a doctor and I was prescribed an antidepressant. On the night of our graduation, I ran into his mother. I was fighting to keep it together. He found me and pulled me in for a hug. My walls were finally crumbling and I felt like I could possibly forgive him. We shared a kiss that promised hope for a relationship again. When we parted and the bitch he had fucked hugged him, I lost it. The memories came crashing back down on me and I realized I would never be able to get past it.

"I went back to my dorm room and tried to drown my sorrows with medication and vodka. Somewhere along the fuzzy way, I thought it would be a good idea to take the entire bottle of pills."

Jackson tensed beside me but I continued. "Before I completely faded away, I called him and told him what I had done. He rushed over and shoved his hand down my throat, causing me to vomit. The doctors told me that, had he not been able to get some of it out of my system, I would have died. My body was so emaciated from not eating that it wouldn't have been able to handle the drug and alcohol concoction well. And even though I feel like I owe him for saving my life, I can't help but feel like I wouldn't have ever fallen to that point if it weren't for his cheating in the first place."

Jackson kissed my temple as the server placed our fajitas in front of us. We started fixing up our fajitas when he spoke. "Are you uncomfortable working with him? We can let him go. I don't want him harassing you," he pronounced, taking a bite.

"No, I feel like we can be civil with each other. Even though I am extremely unhappy with how things turned out, I don't want him to lose his job. I can't help but still care about him. It will just never again be in that way. My heart is too fragile."

He swallowed and looked at me. "He's the reason for your game?" he asked as understanding flooded his features.

I nodded and took a bite of my fajita. Oh my God, it was amazing. "Mmmm, Jackson, this is delicious," I marveled while I chewed.

He laughed and whispered in my ear. "What did I tell you about that moaning? I'm ready to leave the fajitas and have dessert."

His words gave me chills but the fajitas were too good to pass up. "Sorry, Charlie. The fajitas win this time," I teased, laughing and taking another bite.

The rest of our dinner went on amicably as we chatted about easier things. I had fun telling stories about Pepper and Olive. I loved those girls. His stories about him and Jordan were hilarious. From what I gathered, Jackson was the serious one and Jordan was the easygoing brother. He talked fondly of his mother but never mentioned his dad.

"So where is your dad?" I wondered, pushing my plate away. I was completely stuffed. He grumbled but didn't answer right away. I turned to look at him but he avoided my gaze.

"He's dead." That's all he offered. I waited but he didn't elaborate. Hello, Cold Jackson.

I pulled my margarita closer to me and sipped it. The silence dragged on and I was practically squirming in my seat with how uncomfortable it was. Finally, I couldn't stand it any longer. "Jackson, I'm sorry if I hit a nerve. I just wanted to get to know you better. Can you please take me home? I'm tired," I sighed.

As if snapping out of it, he turned to look at me. The pained look on his face told me he still hurt from his father's death. "No. I mean, I'm sorry. I want to spend more time with you. I told you I'm trying. My past isn't wonderful either, Andi. Please spend the night with me. I know this started out as a game but I want to get to know you better too," he pled, pulling me to him.

I turned to study his face for a moment. He looked so broken.

"Okay, but let's swing by my place first so I can pack a bag." I cuddled into him.

He paid our tab and pulled me out of the booth. Leaning over, he kissed me softly on my lips. "Come on. I want to take you somewhere first," he spoke mischievously. I was a sucker for his boyish charm and let him lead me out of the restaurant.

THE NOT-SO-DARK DAYS...

Pepper is hovering. It is so unlike her, but she won't leave me alone. I have to figure out a way to convince her that I'm okay. She won't do anything except go to work, and even then, I practically have to push her out the door.

"Want me to go with you to see Dr. Sweeney?" she asks while she pops her gum at me. "No, Pepper. I can go alone. You haven't visited your dad lately. Maybe you should pay him a visit," I suggest to her.

She pulls her feet out of my lap and sits up. "Andi, are you okay? I mean, I know you seem more like yourself, but I still feel like something is missing. Please tell me if you're not okay. I can't lose my best friend," she confides, eyes tearing up.

I pull her foot back to me and continue to paint her big toe nail. "I'm fine, Pepper. Dr. Sweeney is helping me realize that I am better off without Bray. I've felt the best I have felt in a really long time. I am thankful for your careful watching over me, but I'm going to be okay so you can take it down a few notches. Enjoy your new job at the museum because I'm doing just fine."

She stares at me for a few moments and nods once. Continuing to pop her gum while deep in thought, she lets me finish her toes and never brings it up again.

Chapter SIXTEEN

We drove for about thirty minutes across town. When we got to a charming little street with townhouses adorned with boxed flowers in the windows and ornate light fixtures on the porches, I could hardly contain my excitement.

"Where are we going?" I asked, admiring the homes as we passed. "You'll see," he teased. We sat holding hands until we pulled up in front of one of the homes. He helped me out of the car and we walked up to the front door. Before we could knock, the door flew open, revealing a willowy, dark-haired woman. Her eyes were twinkling when she saw our joined hands and she smiled widely. She was quite beautiful for an older woman.

"Hey, Mom. This is Andi," he greeted, introducing us. My belly fluttered with nervousness at the fact Jackson had brought me to meet his mother. I wish he would have prepared me a little better. She pulled me in for a hug and I couldn't help but giggle at her forwardness. Jordan must get his affectionate personality from his mom.

"It's nice to meet you, Mrs. Compton," I laughed.

"Oh rubbish, call me Trish. You'll make me feel old otherwise," she scolds me.

I chuckle because it reminded me of Jordan yesterday.

"Please, come inside. I just made some coffee and there's a cobbler in the oven." We followed her inside and I admired the way she had decorated her home. It was eccentric but warm, just like Trish. I instantly loved her. My own mother was cold and distant, so I reveled in Trish's attention.

She motioned for us to sit at the small table in the kitchen while she went to the oven to pull out the cobbler. From the smell of it, we were having blackberry. My mouth watered just thinking about it.

Jackson pulled my hand into his lap and winked at me. After Trish scooped ice cream on our cobblers, she brought them to us. Jackson and I dug right in while she poured us some coffee before joining us at the table.

"So tell me a little about yourself, Andi," Trish said.

I closed my eyes when I took a bite because it was absolutely heavenly. "Wow, this is delicious, Trish. Um, let's see. I graduated from Columbia with a Bachelor's in Architecture. I room with my two best friends, Pepper and Olive. This summer I started photographing buildings. I found it very therapeutic. And most obviously, I love food. I woke up one day recently with a new appreciation for it," I remarked, glancing at Jackson, who was listening aptly.

The photography had started when my doctor told me I needed to find something to focus on. A hobby. Nothing had interested me whatsoever. One day, while staring at a beautiful building in the heart of the city, I wished I could freeze the image and commit it to memory. The idea to photograph it had come at that moment and I'd been doing it ever since. I'd even taken an online course to learn more about my thrift store camera.

"Well, Jackie here must be smitten with you. He doesn't bring around girls. Not since Nadia," she confided knowingly.

He stopped her from revealing more, "Mom, Andi doesn't want to hear about past relationships and neither do I."

She frowned but changed the subject. "How's Jordie? He's too busy these days running the firm to come see me. Tell him I'm mad that I haven't seen his precious face in three weeks," she said, apparently miffed.

He laughed at her pouty face. "Don't worry, Mom. I'll take pleasure in telling him that I'm now your favorite," he grinned as he teased her.

After we finished our coffee, Jackson stood up from the table. "Mom, we need to get going. It's late and I need to take Andi home," he lied through his teeth. I rolled my eyes at him but stood up and grabbed hold of his hand.

"Okay, kids, but I want you both over for dinner on Saturday. If you can get your brother to come, please do. Tell him to bring a date," she winked at Jackson.

She hugged us both and walked us to the door. "Hold on a sec!" Trish scurried back into the kitchen and came back with a plate covered with foil and a thermos. "Give this to George." She smiled broadly.

Jackson laughed and shook his head, taking it from her as we headed out the door.

THE NOT-SO-DARK DAYS...

"Andi, I want you to find a new focus. Now that you're out of school and are no longer with Bray, what do you do with your time besides work at the café?" Dr. Sweeney asks me.

I frown because I do absolutely nothing. All I do is replay the events of the last few weeks over and over. When Pepper isn't busy trying to distract me, it is all I can think about. I can hardly sleep because the thoughts consume me. Even though I am no longer distraught, I still can't stop them.

"I don't know what I would do. There isn't much I care about besides Pepper," I tell him honestly.

"I know, Andi, which is why you need to find something. Try some things out. Yoga, kickboxing, reading, pottery, bunko—anything besides what you're doing now. You need to do some soul searching. That's your homework this week. Find something new to think about. I have faith in you that you'll find something.

"Andi, I also want you to try and go on a date. You are a young, attractive woman, and I fear you might end up a little jaded. I'm not saying that you need to go out and find a husband. What I'm saying is that you need to have fun and get out—without Pepper. She's your crutch, and you need to learn to stand on your own again," he told me.

I feel nauseous at the idea of dating, but I nod my head to appease Dr. Sweeney. "Good. Now don't show up next week without a new hobby," he instructs, smiling at me as we conclude our session.

Chapter
SEVENTEEN

When we arrived at the apartment, I made him stay in the car while I ran up to grab my things. Mostly, I wanted to tell the girls about my day without Jackson in earshot.

I walked in the front door to see Olive reading a novel on the couch and Pepper glaring at her laptop. Tossing my keys and purse on the table by the door, I ran over to Olive and kissed her forehead. She smiled at me and blew me a kiss.

Making my way to Pepper, I closed her laptop when I plopped down beside her. She huffed in annoyance but couldn't stop the smile that formed on her face. "What are you so happy about, Andi?" she asked grumpily.

I hugged her and laughed. "I had the weirdest day today. Jackson is outside waiting in the car. I'm going to spend the night with him tonight."

"Hold up. As of yesterday, he was an ass. What's so different about today?" she demanded.

Olive chimed in before I could answer. "Andi, I am just blown away by the fact that you're still seeing the guy and the weekend is over!" She clapped her hands excitedly.

Pepper and I giggled at her. She was so damn cute. "Well, things were looking up this morning. I was in Man-Killer mode and even left the panties at home," I explained, winking at Pepper, who just rolled her eyes. Olive gasped at my proclamation.

I continued my story. "So I got to work and there was a note from Jackson saying we should have lunch in his office again. I was on cloud nine when I went into the conference room to meet the new architect I'll be assisting. Jordan was his normal happy self. But Jackson—his face lit up when he saw me and I almost melted," I tell them dreamily.

"Go on, Jennifer Aniston," Pepper smarted off to me.

"Anyway, the other chair turned and it was—"

Cutting me off, Pepper sneers, "Fucking Brayden."

I nod my head and continue. "So Fucking Brayden got up and hugged me, a little too long for comfort. When we pulled apart, Jackson was killing him with death rays that were shooting from his eyes.

"The meeting was short, but afterwards, Bray stopped at my desk and told me how pretty I was. No surprise there," I winked at them. "I worked and worked until I realized I had been stood up for lunch by Jackson."

"No fucking way. What do you see in that asshole?" Pepper fumed.

I sighed but continued. "Well, Bray realized that I hadn't eaten yet by around two and fetched me a sandwich when I nearly fainted. I ended up dropping the lid and he got an accidental view of the goods." I paused, letting it sink in.

"Oh," Olive whispered.

"God, Andi, you are such a hooch," Pepper scolds me.

I laugh again. "He acted all shocked that I wasn't wearing panties, and Jackson walked up, interrupting his peep show. He looked pissed but then Brayden went off on him for standing me up."

Pepper chuckled because, even though she hates Bray, she liked to see Jackson get the short end of the stick too.

"So he must have felt like an ass because he apologized and disappeared to his office. He called me in there a little while later and fucked me on the credenza."

Olive screeched and Pepper cursed at me.

"And his dick was still in me when Bray knocked on the door. Jackson told him that I'd be right over after we finished up and proceeded to clean me up with Bray on the other side."

Pepper was shaking her head at me, muttering under hear breath, and Olive was fifty shades of crimson.

"So then Fucking Bray decided that he thinks I'm so hot and he wants me so bad. Again, no surprise there. I basically told him to fuck off and bolted from his office.

"Here's where it gets good. So Pepper here canceled on our wine date because she lost her main sponsor. I ran and told Jordan so he would call her and take over the spot."

Pepper interrupted me. "Hold up, you had a hand in that?" she interrogated, agitation lacing her voice.

I nodded beaming, completely proud of saving her ass. "Yep. How'd it go?"

Rolling her eyes, she groaned, "Well, I told him I'd think about it. He's so damn sure of himself, like he knows I'll agree to his requests. I've been trying all night to email other potential sponsors, but most everyone has already made commitments and can't agree to such a costly sponsorship so late in the year. I don't know what I'm going to do."

This time I rolled my eyes, making Olive giggle. "Duh, Pep. You take the Compton Enterprises sponsorship. Really, it's a no-brainer. Now call him and agree!" I griped at her.

She huffed, picked up her laptop, and stalked to her room, ignoring me. I shrugged my shoulders and went into my own room. Quickly, I packed all of my things for tomorrow and headed back out into the living room. I waved to Olive and ran back downstairs to Jackson.

THE NOT-SO-DARK DAYS...

The camera costs just fifty bucks so I buy it. I begin snapping pictures of whatever I can find just to learn how the thing works. Getting the hang of it, I start taking snapshots of buildings in the early morning sun when I am nearly blinded by the reflection of the windows. I also take pictures of them on gloomy days as the rain saturates their surfaces, giving the buildings a gleaming façade.

Photography consumes me. I research it on the internet. I borrow books from the library on the subject. And even participate in an online class to learn more about apertures, ISO, f/stops, and natural light.

Pepper allows me to litter the apartment with photos of the buildings so I can make critiques and choose my favorites. Dr. Sweeney will be so proud. Now, for the whole dating concept...

Chapter
EIGHTEEN

When I climbed back into the car, Jackson was sprawled in his seat, scrolling through his phone. He looked so relaxed and content. Tossing my stuff into the floor, I slammed the car door shut and pounced on him.

He laughed when I started kissing his face all over, trying to be obnoxious. I was in a playful mood this evening. Finally, he palmed my cheeks and held me still so he could kiss my lips. We made out like two teenagers during the short drive to his loft. Helping me out of the car, he grabbed my bags and we practically ran to the elevators. When one opened, he dragged me inside.

Realizing we were alone, he pinned me to the wall and slid his hand up my skirt. I gasped as he slipped a finger inside of me. His mouth found my neck as he pulled his finger in and out at an agonizingly slow speed. I was moaning and begging him to go faster when the doors to the penthouse opened up.

Pulling his finger from me, he took my hand and led me into his loft. Immediately, he jerked off my jacket and began pulling off my camisole. I jerked at his belt, efficiently whipped it off of him, and started working at the button on his pants. When I successfully got the zipper down, I yanked down his pants and boxers, freeing his cock.

Stepping out of them and kicking off his shoes, he reached behind me and slid the zipper to my skirt down, letting it drop to the floor. He also one-handedly unhooked my bra and tossed it away after he pulled it off. We laughed when we realized he was still wearing socks and I still had on my thigh-highs and heels. Kneeling down, he pulled one of the thigh-highs down my leg and off my foot along with my shoe. He repeated his actions on the other side.

On his knees, he pushed me backwards until my back hit the sofa. He spread my legs apart and situated himself between them. I about came unglued when his tongue licked up between my folds before making contact with my clit. My hands grasped his hair as I shivered from the sporadic movement of his tongue. When I would try to jerk away uncontrollably, he would grip my hips and bring them closer to his mouth.

My orgasm shattered through me and my eyes rolled shut from the intense pleasure. "Oh God, Jackson. You make me feel so good," I crooned. Growling, he stood up and turned me around, pushing my top half over the sofa, making my ass point right in the air. I moaned at his sexual roughness. Seeing that I was turned on, he slipped two fingers into me and started stroking my insides. When I started to squirm, he slapped my ass cheek.

The stinging pain only pushed me closer to my next orgasm. I bucked against him and he slapped it again, this time a little harder.

"Oh, fuck! Jackson!" I cried out. I tried to reach behind me to grab his cock but my arms weren't long enough. As he thrusted his fingers harder into me, I started moaning loudly as I felt very near to my release. When his hand slapped me one more time, this time probably leaving a bruise, I screamed and shuddered wildly as my most intense orgasm yet shot through me.

Completely spent, I collapsed against the sofa. Pulling my

wrists behind me, he held them bound together as he poked my entrance with his cock. I nudged him the best I could from my compromised position. Finally, he satisfied us both when he shoved it all the way in. Instinctively, I tried to move my hands but he gripped them tighter as he slammed into me.

"Oh God, Jackson. I'm going to come again!" I shouted as another orgasm pulsed through me. My pussy was clenching around him as his sweaty body pounded against mine. Instantly, his hot climax throbbed into me and I moaned once more. He thrust a couple more times before stopping shakily.

Releasing my wrists, he pulled me back up to a standing position. "Andi, you are fucking amazing. You're like my very own drug. No matter how many times we do this, I can't get enough of you." Then he drew himself from me and popped me on the butt once more for good measure.

I turned around, wrapped my arms around his neck, and kissed him deeply. Leaning away to look him in the eyes, I breathed, "You're pretty addictive yourself." We headed for the shower, leaving our clothes in a heaping pile in the entryway.

After a shower and playing grab ass, we finally crawled into the bed naked. I scooted into the crook of his arm and draped my arm across his chiseled chest. His free hand found its way to my hair and stroked it.

This day had been amazing considering the ex-fiancé I had almost killed myself over had come to work at my new job. My whole weekend game I played was a thing of the past because now I had Jackson.

"So it would appear, Miss Dalton, that you like it a little rough, huh?" Jackson teased, chuckling.

I smiled into his chest. It was the first time I'd ever had a desire to do anything like that but I absolutely loved it. "Mr. Compton, it would appear that you are correct," I purred back.

"Hmmm. Well I can certainly see us having some fun with that," he said in almost a deep whisper.

"Jackie," I joked, using his mother's nickname for him. "But no matter how rough you get, I still have the secret weapon."

He chuckled. "And what would that be?"

I dug my fingers into his side and he rolled out from underneath me and off the bed, escaping my tickling. His boyish laughter boomed across the room. I giggled hysterically at how I could bring Big Bad Jackson to his knees.

Before I had time to respond, he pounced on me, pinning me under his body. He grabbed my wrists again and held them tight above my head with one hand. I wriggled, trying to get free of him, but it was useless. He tried to tickle me but frowned when I didn't respond.

"I'm not ticklish. You'll have to find a different way to get me," I sassed.

Bowing close to my breasts, he kissed one of them softly. I tried to get free but he wouldn't let up. Dipping again, he tongued a portion of my breast, bringing it between his lips. After sucking hard, just to the point of pain, he finally released it. He grinned, admiring his handiwork.

"Do you get off on giving me hickeys?" I questioned, feigning annoyance.

"I'm marking my woman. You're mine," he growled as he suckled another area of my breast. He continued doing this to both breasts until he was satisfied.

Arching an eyebrow at him, I asked, "Are you done yet?"

Shaking his head no, he scooted up to my neck.

"Jackson, don't do it there. Everyone at work will be able to see!" I shrieked, trying to free my wrists again. He laughed and sucked hard, most definitely leaving a hickey. But instead of doing anymore, he pulled away, releasing my wrists.

He looked down into my eyes and we stared at each other. I could see that his guard was down, and he looked so young. It was like he had stripped himself down for me to see his soul. Whatever hid behind those walls was sad. My eyes misted over for a moment.

His mouth found mine and he gently kissed me. He slid himself effortlessly into me and began slowly moving himself in and out. We continued kissing softly. My hands found their way to his back and I rubbed him gently as he continued having his way with me. Our kisses stayed sweet as did his thrusts. When the millionth orgasm of the day came over, I sighed happily into his mouth. He came shortly after into me.

Jackson rested his head against my chest when we were done. "What was that, Andi?" he asked, confused.

I laughed at him while rubbing my hands through his hair. "I think they call it making love," I informed him.

He tensed up and immediately shot off of me. Stalking into the bathroom, he slammed the door behind him.

I couldn't help but feel hurt by his actions. A tear escaped from my eye. After about twenty minutes of waiting for him to emerge from the bathroom, I finally gave up and pulled the covers over me. I fell asleep, trying to ignore the ache in my chest.

THE NOT-SO-DARK DAYS...

"I found photography, Dr. Sweeney," I tell him proudly.

"That's great, Andi. I knew you would find something. Have you been able to channel your thoughts toward photography rather than thinking about Brayden?" he asks me.

"Actually, yes. I haven't thought about him much at all. I may be slightly obsessing over the photography, but it seems to be working," I admit.

"What about the dating?" he asks pointedly.

I wring my hands in my lap, knowing I failed this exercise. "I don't even know where to start. This seems really hard for me," I say honestly.

"I know, Andi. But listen, just go on a date next week. I want you to tell me how you handled it. You know I have complete faith in you. This is a critical step in moving forward with your life."

Sighing, I resign myself to the fact I'll be going on a date this week. It's just homework.

Chapter NINETEEN

When I woke up this morning, Jackson had already left. I felt completely sick to my stomach about the whole thing. We had made love and there was no denying it. He couldn't handle that revelation for some reason, and I intended on pulling it out of him if we ever even had a chance at a real relationship.

After I dressed in another sexy suit, this time wearing panties, I took time straightening my hair and dolling myself up. It seemed that he liked it when I was pretty for him, and I needed him to come back to me.

Emerging from the building, I noticed George waiting by the car. "Mr. Compton asked that I run you to your work," he explained. I nodded and thanked him, allowing him to perform his job. The entire way to work I tried not to think of how Jackson had completely closed himself off to me last night. Was he a commitment-phobe?

It was getting close to eight when we arrived, so I hurried up to the 57th floor. When I got there, I waved to Margie and sat at my desk. Jackson's door was closed but I could hear him talking. My heart did a flip-flop knowing that we were going to have to face each other soon. Did he possibly think that I would be okay with the fact that he had shut me away last night and then left without so much as a goodbye this morning?

Bray walked up to my desk on the way to his office. "Andi, hey. Listen, I'm really sorry about acting like such a dick yesterday. Yes, you are beautiful, but you aren't mine anymore. I understand that. I just hope that we can be friends." He sounded genuinely upset by his actions from the day before.

"Yeah, I'd like that," I told him honestly.

Smiling at my answer, he walked into his office. I powered on my computer to check my emails. There was a reminder already this morning from Bray about the meeting with Mr. Higgins tomorrow that I'd be getting to attend. I was actually looking forward to it. The next email was from Jordan.

Andi,

I'm out of the office until lunch but I wanted to let you know that we got the main sponsorship at the museum. Let's just say that a groveling spice of a woman called me early this morning. I told her I wanted to discuss the parameters of the sponsorship with her over dinner this evening. She fought tooth and nail, but when I told her about the generous donation we were sending with our sponsorship as well, she finally agreed. Ha! ;)

See you soon,

Jordan

I laughed out loud at Jordan's email. It appeared that he had a thing for Pepper, even though she couldn't stand him. Pepper couldn't stand anyone. Props to Jordan for being pushy. Nobody ever got past the frosty exterior with Pepper. But Jordan seemed to be enjoying this personal challenge. The Ice Queen needed to get laid, and who better than the handsome Jordan Compton?

I was still grinning when another email popped into my inbox. Noticing that it was from Jackson, I frowned.

Andi,
You'll need to figure out lunch on your own today.
Jackson

Fuming, I slammed my pen down on the desk. What the hell was his problem? I would confront him but his door was closed and I couldn't be for certain if he had someone in there or not.

Throwing myself into my work, I tuned out all thoughts of Jackson and his drama. By the time lunchtime rolled around, he still hadn't emerged. I was still looking at his office door when Bray came walking out of his own.

"Remember that you promised me lunch today, friend?" Bray reminded be as he flashed his boyish grin. Recalling that I had in fact promised him, I nodded. "Let me grab my purse. I'm at a stopping point," I told him. Once I had my purse, we walked to the front door together. Throwing one last glance at Jackson's office door, I gasped when I saw him watching us leave and he looked pissed. Fuck him.

"This place has the best Indian tacos," Bray stated, pointing at the menu.

The smell of the restaurant made my stomach groan with joy. "Sounds good. I'll have that and a tea."

After the server took our order and brought us our drinks, we started chatting about easy topics. He'd been working at another firm since right after graduation. The Compton brothers had actually sought him out to work at their firm because he had built a quick reputation of being an excellent architect. They had offered to pay him twice as much as he was making at the previous place, so of course he accepted.

He asked about Pepper and what she was doing these days. I told him all about the museum and even a little bit about Jordan attempting to take her out, even if he had to sneak the date in. "That's comforting. I actually thought he had a thing for you yesterday by the way he had his hand on your leg," he admitted.

"I think he's just an affectionate person. It really just seemed friendly to me," I said truthfully.

"Well, I wasn't the only one to think that. Jackson seemed like he was ready to throw him out the window. It's obvious there is something going on between you and him," he conveyed, waiting for my confirmation.

"Yeah, well it's complicated," I muttered, trying to change the subject.

"Complicated, how?" he inquired. Subject unsuccessfully avoided.

"Well, some moments we have a really great connection, but then in an instant he's cold and aloof. I don't understand how he switches back and forth so easily. My feelings remain the same so I end up hurt and confused when he flips the switch." I frowned.

Bray reached across and took my hand. I wanted to jerk it away, but it really just was a friendly move. "He better find out real quick what he wants because you don't deserve to be dragged around like that." That was interesting coming from him, but at least he was trying to protect me.

Pulling my hand back into my lap, I agreed, "I know. I'm finally in a place where I can be happy with myself since the 'incident'. If he can't get on the same page as me, it won't bode well for my psyche. It's already fragile as it is."

Bray flinched at the word "incident" but tried to play it off. It was incredibly strange to be having a conversation about my new love interest with my ex-fiancé. Pepper and Olive would have a new story to hear this evening. It seemed my life is wildly entertaining.

The server dropped off the food and left us again. We dug in, effectively ending the conversation about Jackson. The tacos were amazing. I might have just found a new favorite restaurant.

Bray started laughing at me as I went on and on about how good my food was. The rest of the meal went on just fine. As unusual as the situation was, I had missed the friendly banter we had always shared. Perhaps being friends with Bray wasn't the most horrible idea of all. We had to work together, so the least we could do was get along.

Before I could pull out my wallet to pay my portion of lunch, Bray had already handed the server a handful of cash. "Bray, you didn't have to do that. I'll pay next time," I admonished him sternly, mostly for the fact that I in no way wanted this to be considered a date.

He chuckled, "Sounds like a plan, Andi. It was the least I could do after...well, after everything I did to you." His eyes turned serious as he looked over at me. "Andi, I will forever be sorry for how I treated you. Every day I'm thankful that you didn't die from the overdose. Everything about our breakup and the event that caused it made me rethink my life. I will value my next relationship more seriously because of everything that happened to you as a result of my actions. Can you forgive me, Andi?"

He'd apologized so many times before, but this one seemed the most genuine. Maybe because it wasn't just a ploy to get us back together? I smiled at him and nodded.

"Yes, Bray. I forgive you," I responded, standing from the booth.

He mirrored my actions and then pulled me in for a hug. It was brief but comforting. Little by little, my heart and mind were healing.

The whole way back we chatted about baseball. Bray had never wanted to pursue it outside of college. It had always just been a means to pay for college.

Once we arrived on our floor, Bray hurried to his office, remembering a client he needed to call. I hesitantly walked over to my desk after noticing that Jackson's door was open. When I stepped in front of his door, he was staring right out at me. Our eyes locked in a moment of intensity.

Neither of us said anything but we didn't back away either. Finally, deciding to mess with him, I turned away and bent over to drop my purse in my desk drawer, hesitating for a few seconds longer than it should have taken.

He cursed under his breath, but I still heard it. Ignoring him, I sat down at my desk and began checking my emails. There were a few that needed immediate attention and I replied to those. I was finishing up with those when a new one pinged my inbox.

Andi,
Did you fuck him?
Jackson

My blood boiled at his question. He thought he could ignore me all night and most of today but then accuse me of sleeping with Bray like suddenly he cared. Screw him!

Before I would allow myself to cool off or even look at him, I sent him a reply.

Jackie,
What's it to you?
The Office Slut

Firing it off at him, I sat quietly for a moment, trying to collect myself. I was furious with him and his insinuations.

Bray decided to walk up to my desk about that moment. He held out a folder to me. "This is the Higgins file I started. You might want to briefly look it over so you'll have an idea about the proposal and his business history."

Reaching up, I grabbed for the file, but Bray snatched my wrist in his hand.

"What the fuck is this, Andi? Did he do this to you?" he asked angrily, jerking his head towards Jackson's office.

Oh shit. My wrist had bruising all around it from Jackson gripping me last night. I wasn't sure how I was going to explain this to Bray.

"Um, we..." I trailed off, not knowing how to explain this to him. He was glaring at me so I had to at least try. "It was consensual," I finally admitted, looking down at my keyboard. He let go of my wrist and I pulled it back to me.

Turning on his heel, he stalked into Jackson's office and slammed the door. Shit! I jumped up to try and stop what was about to happen. Jackson and Bray were chest to chest by the time I ran in there.

Bray had his finger in Jackson's face. "You hurt her and I will fucking kill you. She is fragile and you keep fucking with her. What the fuck's wrong with you?"

They were pretty evenly matched size-wise so this could get bad. Jackson was pretty much touching Bray's nose with his own when he growled, "It's your fucking fault that she's fragile in the first place. I hope you live with the guilt that you almost fucking killed her so you could get your dick wet in some whore."

Tears welled up in my eyes when I realized half of the office was standing in the doorway, watching the drama unfold, and hearing my dark secrets that I would have rather have kept quiet from them.

Jackson shoved Bray away from him, making him stumble backwards into me. I fell to the floor on my ass with a thud that practically knocked the breath out of me.

About that time, Jordan's voice boomed, "Bray, get back to your office! Jackson, go home!" He jerked Bray's arm and pushed him towards the door. Kneeling beside, he put his arm around me. "Andi, are you okay?" he questioned.

"Don't fucking touch her, Jordan!" Jackson roared, yanking his arm off of me. Jordan jumped up, furious with Jackson, and physically dragged him out of the office. This was so bad. I could hear Margie telling everyone to get back to their desks as Jordan forced Jackson out of the building.

Bursting into tears on the floor in Jackson's office, Jordan came back in, shutting the door behind him. He pulled me up and led me to one of the chairs, still scowling from having manhandled his brother. "Are you okay?" he asked again, sitting in the chair beside me.

I just shook my head and buried it in my hands as the tears flowed continuously.

He patted my knee, trying to comfort me. "Andi, my brother has issues. I can see that you guys have something going on. Not to mention, I heard it all yesterday through my office wall," he chuckled under his breath.

I groaned in embarrassment, realizing my boss had heard me having sex with his brother in the next room while at work. Could this day get any worse?

"He doesn't do relationships very well. That's why I am surprised that you guys have managed to keep up whatever it is you're doing as long as you have. It's unlike him to stay interested for so long. And boy is he jealous. I also know about your past with Bray. He told me yesterday. And with what they argued about a few minutes ago, it appears that you are caught in the middle of two men who want to protect you but have a terrible way of showing it," he observed.

"Jordan, I am so, so sorry for this. I am horribly embarrassed," I whimpered tearfully, looking up at him.

He smiled at me. "Andi, no worries. He's my brother. I'm used to him, and so is the rest of the office. He's hard to figure out because he's all over the place with his emotions. If you have the patience for him, I bet he'll come around eventually."

"I don't know if I can handle it. I mean, I really like him. He can be funny, sweet, and caring. But the next moment, he's so distant or he acts like he forgets about me. I don't understand it. Do you think he's as interested in me as I am him? I'll be honest, I'm too weak to be played around with."

Jordan looked at me thoughtfully. "He'll come around, Andi. I can see that he really likes you, but he's struggling with some demons from his past. Why don't you go on home? You've had a rough afternoon. Everyone can start fresh tomorrow with better frames of mind."

"Thank you, Jordan. You're quite possibly the best boss ever. I hope your dinner tonight goes well with Pepper. She's worth the fight too, you know."

He smiled and winked at me. He knew she was. I could tell by the look in his eyes.

I stood up from my chair so I could pack my things and leave. Jordan pulled me in for a hug. Laughing into his chest, I said, "By the way, you need to visit your mother. She misses you."

He pulled away and looked at me. "He took you to see Mom?" he asked, clearly bewildered.

"Yeah, and she's quite adorable. You should be ashamed of yourself for not visiting more often," I scolded him.

Shaking his head, he chuckled, "That's proof right there, Andi. You're only the second girl he has ever brought home to Mom. He likes you."

I smiled at him and left the office.

Everyone that was staring at me as I walked out quickly looked down, trying to look busy. I snatched my purse and bag, heading out for the day. Margie waved at me on the way out.

On the elevator ride down, I frowned at how the day had gone. It really had been an awful day. I knew Bray was trying to protect me. So was Jackson. But they had a terrible way of showing it.

When I stepped out of the building and saw Jackson's car, I quickly made my way down the sidewalk and away from it in case he was inside. I would just catch a cab at the next intersection.

Footsteps sounded behind me before I could get very far. "Andi, wait!" Jackson's voice shouted from behind me.

Ignoring him, I kept walking speedily away. His arm suddenly snaked around my middle and stopped me in my tracks. He put his nose to the back of my head and inhaled.

"Get in the car, please."

THE NOT-SO- DARK DAYS...

After several awkward dating attempts from using a dating website, I finally decide to just hit the bar and see if I can find someone that way.

Pepper and I walk into a dance club, not straying far from each other. Thankfully she isn't making me go alone, even though she hates this sort of scene. I'm nervously looking for a place to sit when someone touches my arm.

"Where's your boyfriend?" a deep voice asks me. I turn to see a good-looking guy not much older than me smiling down at me.

"I don't have one," I tell him, lifting my chin in an attempt to appear more confident than I feel.

"Hmmm, maybe we can fix that," he teases. "I'm Eric."

Taking his hand, I say, "Andi." I grin at him because this good-looking guy seems interested in me.

We spend the next couple of hours dancing, talking over the music, and drinking. He invites me to his place.

"Sounds fun. Let me tell my friend," I tell him.

The prospect of what's about to happen has butterflies swarming in my stomach.

I turn to Pepper. "Pep, I am going home with Eric."

She frowns at me. "I don't like this, Andi, but if this is what helps you heal, then fine. You better call me if things get weird and I'll be there in a snap to get you." I nod and we hug goodbye.

Eric and I take a cab to his apartment nearby. We can hardly keep our hands off of each other as we go inside. Everything happens quickly, and the next thing I know, I've just slept with a complete stranger. Oddly enough, I don't feel bad about it. In fact, I think it may just be a one-night thing with this guy because he's already getting on my nerves with all his talk about Call of Duty.

When he falls asleep, I slip out and catch a cab home. I feel powerful for the first time in weeks.

Chapter
TWENTY

His arm around my belly sent chills down my spine. He made me crazy in both a good and bad way. I was so upset with him right now, but my body was betraying me as I melted into his arms. Annoyed with myself for what I was about to do, I nodded.

He squeezed me and kissed my hair. I couldn't help but feel a flutter of excitement and happiness now that Hot Jackson was back.

I allowed him to help me into the car, tossing my bags on the floor. He slid in beside me closed the door behind him. George began driving us to who knows where.

Still not wanting to look at him, I played with the hem of my skirt that had ridden pretty high from sitting in the low seats. Jackson leaned his mouth to my ear and whispered, "I'm sorry." Even though his hot breath tickled me and sent a shudder down my body, it wasn't enough. Actions and words were two different things.

Realizing just how upset I was, he pulled away one of my hands from my skirt and lifted it to his mouth. He held it to his lips and gently kissed it. It was so intimate and spoke volumes.

I finally decided to look at him. The same heart-wrenching soul I had seen last night while making love with him was staring back at me with sad brown eyes. A tear slipped out and over my cheek. He gently wiped it away. Not being able to stop myself, I leaned forward and touched my lips to his. He kissed me sweetly, as if he were trying to express his apology through his lips.

We softly explored one another's mouths with our tongues. His hands settled on my upper thighs, rubbing circles with his thumbs while he kissed me. I threaded my fingers through his hair, massaging his scalp with my fingertips.

He broke our kiss when we came to a stop in front of my apartment. "Come inside with me?" I asked. I was feeling vulnerable and needed more of his touch to comfort me. He nodded and we headed upstairs.

Once in the apartment and I had dropped my stuff on the sofa, I took his hand, leading him into my room. After we made it to my room and shut the door, I unbuttoned my jacket and pulled it off. Jackson followed suit with his own. I peeled off my camisole, leaving myself in a sexy white lace bra, and kicked off my heels. He quickly undid the buttons on his dress shirt and threw it aside.

Walking up to me, he reached behind me and unclasped my bra. He slipped it off and his hands made their way to the zipper on my skirt, undoing it as well. The skirt fell to the floor, and I stood before him in my barely-there matching white lace panties and thigh-highs.

"You're absolutely beautiful, Andi. Every time I see you, I can't take my eyes off of you. I'm an asshole and don't deserve someone like you. But I still want you. I still want you to want me," he confessed. His face didn't have his normal guard up and he seemed so fragile. What was behind the tough exterior? I needed to find out.

He unbuttoned his pants and slipped them off along with his boxers, socks, and shoes. Instead of letting me take off the stockings or panties, he led me to the bed.

Leaning over, he brought his lips to mine again. Melting in his sweet kisses, I wrapped my arms around him, squeezing his bare bottom. I could feel him harden between us, making me want him so badly. He lowered us onto the bed and our kisses intensified. I kept pulling him to me and grinding my hips up to him, letting him know what I wanted.

Taking the hint, he sat up and slipped my panties off. Lowering himself back over me, he positioned his cock at my entrance and pushed it in.

I moaned loudly because he always felt so good and we fit together perfectly. He started a rhythm that matched our kissing and I tensed up as an orgasm neared. One of his hands slid up and caressed my breast. My pants intensified and I cried out as electricity coursed through my body. I shuddered beneath him, and he followed quickly behind me, coming into me.

Collapsing on me so our chests pressed together, he peered down at me. "Making love," he stated. Not a question but a statement. I smiled, nodding. Pecking me on the lips really quickly, he drew himself out and stretched beside me. I curled into him, tracing the ridges of his stomach muscles with my finger.

"So what happened last night?" I murmured, not looking up at him. He didn't speak right away and a tear slipped out of the corner of my eye. I feared we were about to have a repeat from the night before.

His hand gently tugged my chin up to look at him. "Last night was a mistake," he began. When my chin started to quiver, he continued quickly. "It was a mistake because I freaked out. You're not her, so I need to trust you because you haven't given me any reason not to." I didn't really understand who "she" was, but I had a feeling it was the Nadia Trish had spoken of.

"Jackson, you really hurt me. I felt so rejected when you didn't come to bed last night and were gone this morning. I have no idea what we're doing here. This all goes against everything I have trained myself to do in the past five months. But one thing's for sure. I don't want it to go away. Nothing feels right unless I am with you."

I continued. "And then you avoided me all day, further hurting my feelings. You made me feel like I had done something wrong. After lunch with Bray, you basically called me a whore and that fucking hurt, Jackson. From the moment I heard your voice, you're all I can think about. No one else."

He crashed his lips to mine, nicking my lip with his teeth. The taste of blood seemed to jolt us alive, because the next moment he had me flipped over on my hands and knees. He lined himself behind me and slammed into my pussy that still dripped from his orgasm moments ago.

My fingers grasped the blankets as he pounded into me from behind. His fingers digging into my hips agitated my bruises from last night but I didn't care. We were amazing together.

His hand latched on to my hair and yanked my head back. The other hand slipped over my clit and started rubbing it furiously. My climax tore through me, and when my head dropped down, he jerked my hair, pulling it back where he wanted it. The sting from my hair that was wrapped up in his fist only intensified the orgasm pulsing through me and I screamed his name in delight. He poured into once me more, pumping until he was empty and I was full.

Before I had time to even think, he slipped himself out of me and chuckled. "Now that was fucking," he smirked as he headed for the shower. Indeed it was, Mr. Compton. Indeed it was.

THE NOT-SO-DARK DAYS...

Craig has me bent over his kitchen table, fucking me like a madman. This is day three of our little escapade. He's a great lay but rules are rules. Soon after he comes into me, he slips himself out and yanks off the condom, tossing it into the trash. I pull up my panties and readjust my dress. The tattoos across his sculpted chest are hot as hell and I'll miss them.

Walking to the front door, I say, "I had fun, Craig. Thanks for a good time."

Before I can make it out, he grabs hold of my hand. "Wait, Andi. I think things are going pretty well. Let's go out tomorrow. When I agreed to a weekend of fun, I didn't think you meant it. What chick would ever actually be serious about something like that?"

Here it is—the part that I hate. It seems like this happens every weekend, if they even make it three days. "Craig, I'm all for fun, but the rules are three days. You agreed to it and now it's over," I remind him, jerking my hand away from his grasp.

"You're a fucking bitch!" he yells at me, kicking the door behind me. I jump, startled at his reaction. Pepper always warns me that I'm going to get myself in over my head one day. Shit, I hope today's not that day.

Glaring back at him, I sling my purse over my shoulder and stalk out of his apartment before he has time to kick anything else. Asshole. He knew the rules going into it.

Chapter TWENTY -ONE

After we rinsed off quickly in the shower and dressed, we went to the living room to decide where we should go.

Olive was perched on the edge of the couch filing her nails. "Hey, guys," she looked up and smiled at me. I hadn't really seen either her or Pepper very much lately.

"Olive, you should come with us. We'll go have dinner, the three of us. Please," I begged her.

Normally, she might have said no, but I think she missed me, and I was taking advantage of that fact. Indecision crossed her features but she finally agreed. "Okay, let me put on some shoes." She skipped off to her room.

"What's on the menu for tonight?" I asked Jackson.

"Well, I'd say you except you invited your friend to dinner, so I guess we'll just have to settle for sushi," he teased. I kissed him a little too long on the lips because Olive cleared her throat when she walked into the room.

I laughed and pushed away from him grabbing Olive's hand.

Together, the three of us left for dinner.

The entire drive to the restaurant, Olive twisted her hands nervously. Jackson probably couldn't tell that she was anxious about going out, but I knew she was. Poor girl never went anywhere hardly. Drake had really messed her up. *Maybe I should drag her to Dr. Sweeney's with me one day.*

We were seated right away by a picture window overlooking the busy street. I sat beside Jackson in the booth and his hand settled on my thigh. There'd be no action at this booth since I'd changed into jeans earlier. Bummer.

After we ordered, Olive told us about a gig she had coming up. "Saturday I'm going to be doing a photo shoot for Express. I'm really nervous because it's going to get a lot of exposure. Something like this could thrust me into a whole new realm, one I may not be ready for," she admitted worriedly, chewing on her bottom lip.

"Olive, you'll do fine. You are stunning, and by not letting the world see you, you're doing them all a disservice," I praised, earning a smile from her.

"Who's your agent?" Jackson asked, sipping his drink.

"Vance Fleck. He wants me to do more than just a random photo shoot here and there. Vance says that I've got the exotic look that so many companies are after. I just don't know. It kind of freaks me out. Drake is so involved with photographing live events that I'm afraid my chances of running into him will be much greater. I can't run into him. Ever," she confided cryptically as she shivered.

"What did he do to you?" Jackson questioned, concern written all over his face.

"He was abusive in more ways than you can count. I'm thankful every day I got away when I did. Running into him would mean fearing for my life again," she frowed. Again. Fearing for her life—again. I hope she never ran into him either.

Jackson looked angry at the thought of anyone wanting to hurt sweet Olive. I couldn't agree more. The server placed our plates in front of us and I smiled happily, even clapping my hands together. Jackson and Olive chuckled at my excitement over food.

"You're obsessed with food. How come you're so skinny?" he teased.

Ignoring his question, I popped a spicy tuna roll into my mouth. "This is so good. I could eat here every night," I told them after I swallowed it.

"You practically do, Andi. Who are you trying to kid?" Olive inquired, busting me.

I rolled my eyes at her. "Not every night. More like every other night," I sassed.

After we finished our meal, Jackson spoke as he handed his card over to the server. "You ladies want to go visit Ian over at the bar and have a couple of drinks? It isn't very busy on Wednesday nights," he asked, looking at Olive. She squirmed a little at his request but almost imperceptibly nodded her head yes.

I grinned at her and squeezed Jackson's thigh letting him know this was a big deal for her. His hand found mine and squeezed it back. After he got his card back, we all made our way back to the car, where George waited for us.

The ride to the bar was quick and gave Olive little time to back out. Once we arrived, I held on to her hand, attempting to give her the support she needed for this outing.

The bar was slow just like Jackson promised and we found the booth we sat in yesterday.

Ian came over and slid into the booth next to Olive, making her light brown cheeks turn red. "Yo, Tina! I'm taking a break to visit with some friends. Take over for me. Can you send out some shots too? Surprise us," he hollered to the dark-haired waitress. She gave him the thumbs up and set off to make the drinks. "Hello, Miss Olive, it's so nice to see you again," he grinned at her.

"Hi, Ian," she spoke shyly.

Turning to Jackson, he said, "Hey, man. How's it going?"

They launched into a conversation about what bands would be at the bar over the weekend and how the bar was doing financially.

I mouthed to Olive, "Are you okay?" She nodded and formed a small smile on her face.

When the shots arrived, we all downed them quickly. Tina brought us a few more after that. Olive and I were getting pretty giggly. I was having fun teasing Jackson about his serious nature. When he'd scowl at me, I'd tickle him and he'd laugh like a little boy. It was hysterical, and Olive agreed, which only egged me on more. Ian was watching her like she was on the menu, which was the least bit unnerving.

When he slung his arm around her and whispered into her ear, she shot me a look of panic. Before I could even tell him to back off, Jackson had already shot out of the booth and was dragging Ian along with him.

"What the fuck, man?" he spat as Jackson hauled him away from the table. Olive and I didn't stick around for the argument, and we hurried out to the car hand in hand. Once we hopped into the car, I drew her in for a hug.

"Are you okay?" I asked her.

"Yeah, I totally freaked. I'm sorry," she sniffled. "That was probably normal but I don't do well with that sort of thing."

"What did he say?" I questioned, wanting to know what gave her that look of terror.

"All he said was,"—she paused for a moment—"you're going to be effing screaming my name later, baby."

I tried to hide my smile when she said "effing." She didn't cuss like a sailor like Pepper and I did.

"Honey, he was flirting, but I can see how that would freak you out a little."

She nodded and looked sad. "I want to like him, but I think I'm ruined. There just wasn't a spark. He's really good-looking but there isn't anything there."

"Olive, it's okay. You had fun tonight. I'm proud of you for being brave and going with us. Pepper is going to shit a brick when she finds out she missed it!"

Olive and I giggled as Jackson slipped into the car. "Olive, I want to apologize on behalf of my friend. He just says whatever he wants whenever he wants. Blame it on his Irish blood. He's a major player so you'd be wise just staying friends with him."

She smiled at him. "Don't worry, Jackson. I'll stick with being his friend. Thanks for looking out for me. You're a good guy." She patted his knee. His features darkened when she called him a "good guy," and I absolutely noticed it when it happened. Would I ever peel back his layers?

Leaning over, he whispered into my ear, "Want to come home with me?" I nodded and he kissed my temple.

"I need to grab some more clothes first. You can help me pack," I told him, winking.

Once at the apartment, the three of us made our way upstairs. When I unlocked the door and flung it open, my mouth dropped as I saw Pepper fly off the couch with a guilty-as-hell look on her face. None other than Jordan Compton sat on the couch, legs kicked up on the coffee table, with a laptop sitting on his thighs.

Clearly they were working, but Pepper looked extremely guilty, which meant we had almost interrupted something. Damn!

"Hey, guys. Uh, Jordan, er, Mr. Compton and I are going over the sponsorship for the museum," she stuttered unconvincingly.

Jackson boomed with laughter at Jordan when he looked at Pepper with a raised eyebrow like even he was having a hard time believing what she was saying. She looked completely flustered, which caused me and Olive to giggle at her.

"Ugh! We were just working!" she cried, scowling at all of us, especially Jordan. "You people suck."

Jackson of course would choose this moment to make her even more uncomfortable. "Our mother is having dinner at her house Saturday, Pepper. Would you care to join us? I'd ask Olive too but she has a modeling job."

Pepper glanced over at Jordan, who winked at her. She blushed momentarily but regained her composure quickly. "I'm busy," she blurted.

At the same time, Olive and I shouted at her, "Liar!"

She glared at both of us but it only made us laugh harder at her. Apparently we were all enjoying this. Well, except Pepper of course.

"Fine, but I'll find my own ride there and I am not going as your date, Jordan," she huffed to him.

"Come here. I want to show you something," he told her, eyes full of mischief. She hesitantly went over to him and sat down.

He pointed to the screen, and when she leaned over to look at it, he slipped an arm around her and planted a sloppy kiss on her cheek. She shrieked and tried to get away but he just laughed and held her there.

Jackson reached over and grabbed the laptop before it hit the floor. When Jordan stuck his tongue in her ear, she threw out a string of cusswords, but he still wouldn't let her go. At this point, everyone was laughing hysterically except for Pepper.

She was trying to stay pissed, but with Jordan, who was always smiling, it was hard even for her, the Ice Queen. He leaned over and whispered something into her ear that made her jaw drop before he finally released her.

Whatever it was must have infuriated her because she hauled off and punched him in the stomach, effectively knocking the breath out of him.

Jackson grabbed my hand and dragged me into my room much to my dismay. I was enjoying the show, but it was clear he wanted to make a show of our own. Kicking the door closed behind us, he tossed me on my bed and we did exactly that.

THE NOT-SO-DARK DAYS...

*"You're going to get crabs or Chlamydia or Gonorrhea or—"
Pepper drones on but I slap a hand over her mouth.*

*"Pep, I use condoms. Chill. You need to get out more. When
was the last time you got laid anyway?" I really want to know the
answer.*

*"Ugh, don't change the subject. I'm serious, I worry about
you. Does Dr. Sweeney know that your idea of 'dating' really
means fucking anything with a penis?" She pops her gum at me.*

*"No, Pepper. Dr. Sweeney and I don't get into the specifics.
He says he's proud of me for dating," I sass back at her.*

*"Does he know your vag gets more business than a Seven
Eleven with buy-one-get-one-free slushies?" She cocks an eyebrow
at me.*

*"That's just gross. You can't compare my vag to a
convenience store!"*

"But it's so convenient," she laughs.

*I stick my tongue out at her. Pepper the bitch. Pepper, my best
friend.*

Chapter TWENTY-TWO

We walked in the next morning holding hands. People weren't going to know what to think about us. Bray was asking Margie something when he saw us. He took one look at our hands, shook his head, and stormed into his office. *Whatever, Bray.*

Jackson glared after him. "Asshole," he muttered under his breath.

"Jackson! That's enough. You guys need to get along," I chided him. He mumbled something and walked into his office. Before I could power on the computer, Bray was standing over my desk.

"You ready to go the meeting?" he questioned, no hint of a smile on his face.

"Uh, sure. Let me tell Jackson really quick."

I stepped into Jackson's office, and he motioned for me to close the door.

"Jackson, I'm about to leave for that meeting with Bray. I just wanted to let you know."

He stood and then stalked over to me. I could feel the heat of his chest close to mine. His hand slipped under my skirt and I gasped. Growling, he slid his finger over my silky panties, rubbing my sensitive area. "Just making sure you were wearing panties. I don't want Bray getting anymore sneak peeks."

I melted to his touch. Any time his hands were on me, I couldn't help but ignore everything around me. The silk of my panties were getting wet as he continued to stroke me under my skirt. I was about to come when someone knocked on the other side of the door.

"We need to leave, Andi." Bray sounded agitated from the other side.

"She'll be out in thirty seconds," Jackson barked to him as he continued working me beneath my skirt. When I felt my orgasm crash over me and a moan start to escape my lips, Jackson smothered it with his own lips, kissing me as I rode it the rest of the way.

When he was sure I was finished, he pulled away. "You're my girl, not his," he growled. As if I needed reminding. He pecked me on the lips and then opened the office door. Bray stood on the other side, arms crossed.

"Come on, Bray. Let's go," I spoke evenly, trying not to sound flustered. He led the way out the door and I smiled as I felt Jackson's eyes on my ass as we left.

The Higgins office was just a few blocks away so the cab ride was short. I was still peeved at Bray for going ballistic on Jackson yesterday afternoon, so I wasn't in the mood for small talk. Finally needing to break the silence, he cleared his throat and spoke.

"Andi, I'm sorry about losing my shit yesterday. I saw the bruises on your wrist and I flipped out. The thought of him hurting you pissed me off. It went further than it should have because quite frankly he's an ass and I'm already sick of him," he said gruffly.

"Well, you two guys need to get along if you plan on working there for much longer. He's part owner of the company. You're just an employee. If you piss him off too bad, he'll fire you," I explained.

"Nah, he's bound by contract. I signed for a year. He isn't that stupid, especially with all of the lawsuits he's already involved in."

Lawsuits? "What lawsuits?" I asked, my curiosity piqued.

"Nothing. Just forget about it. So Mr. Higgins is an old man— a dirty old man. That's the real reason I brought you," he admitted, face displaying a shit-eating grin.

"What? You set me up, you asshole!"

He laughed. "Yeah, I figured we might land the account if you came along. He'll be so busy looking at those long legs that he won't care about much else."

I punched him in the arm and rolled my eyes. "You're so full of shit."

We got to the conference room a few minutes late. When we walked in, I realized Bray was not full of shit when the old man unabashedly checked me out. Good thing Jackson wasn't here.

"Mr. Greene, so nice to have you. And who's the exquisite woman you have with you?" he questioned Bray like I was just a trophy rather than a person. I had to try really hard not to roll my eyes.

"This is my friend and co-worker, Andi."

I shook Mr. Higgins's hand, and when he held on to it for a moment too long, I refrained from jerking it from his grasp. He finally let go, and I took the seat next to him after he motioned to it.

Bray got right down to business and presented his information to Mr. Higgins, who was too busy looking at the hemline of my skirt to pay attention to anything he was saying. Bray winked at me as he slipped the contract in front of Mr. Higgins, who reluctantly peeled his eyes away from my legs.

Scribbling away his signature, he returned his gaze back to my legs. Bray was definitely going to get an earful the moment we left this godforsaken room.

Bray was stacking up the papers to put them back in the folder when the old man licked his lips. My anger boiled over and I snapped.

"Take a picture. It'll last longer," I spat through my teeth.

His eyes jerked up to mine and he guffawed loudly. "Mr. Greene, you have quite the feisty secretary here," he grinned over at Bray.

He just nodded and smiled, shaking Mr. Higgins's hand. "Good doing business with you, Mr. Higgins. We'll be in touch," he promised, heading for the door.

Mr. Higgins's eyes perused my body once more before I was able to get out of that conference room. That was absolutely the most disgusting man I had ever met.

Bray got the silent treatment until were downstairs and outside.

"You are such a jerk! I was your distraction for that pervert!" I yelled at him.

He doubled over in laughter. "You should have seen your face. I thought you were going to deck him."

We chose to walk back to our building, enjoying the sunshine. Plus, it allowed more time for me to gripe at him about the whole situation.

Once we got back up to the offices, I noticed that Jackson's door was shut. Giving Bray one more "go to hell" look, I sat down to check my emails. There was one from Pepper that made me smile.

Andi,

I miss my best friend. Want to grab lunch today? I have to have your impossibly difficult boss Jordan sign some documents for the sponsorship, so I'll be in today. If I don't get hauled off for clawing his eyes out, then let's have a lunch date.

Pep

I grinned, no longer annoyed with the meeting with Mr. Higgins, as I typed her a response that I would go with her. We hadn't seen much of each other lately, and I missed her badly.

"Is Jackie in today?" a voiced purred behind me. Something about the sensual voice and the way she had said his nickname that only his mother called him made my stomach churn. Swiveling in my chair, I took in the sight of a stunning woman. She was runway-model tall with impossibly long legs jetting out from her tailored coat. Her legs were tan and shimmered in the light. I was mesmerized by them.

The tap of her manicured nails on my desk pulled me from my gawking at her legs. Her breasts were practically spilling out of the top of her coat. She had large breasts for someone of her size, making me think they were fake. Breasts that perfect had to be fake. Her long, dark hair hung in delicate waves, framing her gorgeous face. Pursing her pink lips together, she waited for me to answer. I was immediately intimidated by her.

"Um, I'm not sure. I just got back from a meeting. Let me check. Can I tell him who's here to see him?" I inquired, wanting to know the name of the beautiful woman who was about to meet with my man.

"Nadia Compton," she answered, narrowing her eyes at me.

Jerking my head towards her, I felt my entire body go cold. My jaw dropped and I stuttered a bit, not knowing what to say to her.

"I'm his wife." She watched me for my reaction, but I didn't give her the satisfaction of one. I only smiled at her as I stood to inform Jackson that she was here. This woman was a calculating bitch. It was written all over her face. *Jackson's fucking wife.*

Snapping out of my shock, I stalked over to Jackson's door and peeked my head in. He beamed at me, further pissing me off.

Smiling sweetly back at him, I reported, "Your wife is here to see you."

His smile fell as a look of horror crossed his face. "Fuck!" he burst out, rubbing his hands across his jawline. "Andi, it isn't what you think. We're going through a really nasty divorce. I'm sorry I didn't tell you. I promise we'll talk about this after she leaves."

I curtly nodded at him, lips pressed into a thin line before turning to Nadia. "He'll see you now Mrs. Compton," I seethed.

Winking at me, she sashayed into the office, shutting the door behind her.

That woman was a bitch. I could see why he was divorcing her.

When two hands covered my eyes from behind, I laughed because I could recognize that peppermint gum smell from anywhere.

"Pepper!"

She laughed and pulled her hands away, hopping on the top of my desk. Her hair was pulled up in a standard messy bun that was unique to Pepper. Today, something was different though. From behind her glasses I could see that she had on eye makeup, giving her already pretty eyes a more dramatic look.

"Pepper, oh my goodness, you're wearing makeup!" I exclaimed.

She rolled her eyes at me. "It's not a big deal. I do that sometimes, you know."

But I did know and she did not do that sometimes. She could lie, but I saw right through it. Pepper was seeing Jordan and she wanted to look pretty. The smile on my face grew.

"Did you already visit with Jordan?" I asked.

"Nah, he isn't back yet. He said he had a meeting and he'd probably be done by now but I guess it's gone over. That's okay. We'll grab lunch and I'll see him after."

"It's a date. Let me tell Jackson I'm going. He's in there with his bitchy soon-to-be ex-wife. You just missed the bitch and all of the awkwardness."

I stood up to go tell him when Bray came out of his office. "Hey, Pepper, how's it going?" he asked, walking over to her. She hated Bray but chatted with him anyway.

I flung open the door to Jackson's office without knocking. Bitch Nadia needed to know that she couldn't just keep me out where Jackson was concerned. He was with me now.

But my mind had trouble comprehending what I saw, and it blinked with flashbacks to when I had walked in on Bray cheating on me last spring.

Bitch Nadia stood completely naked, coat crumpled on the floor behind her. Her hands had a grip around his tie and she and Jackson were kissing. His hands were on her shoulders.

"Holy shit," I heard Pepper gasp from behind me. Bray's strong arms hooked around my waist and pulled me from the scene in the office, closing the door between us and them.

From the other side, I heard Jackson cursing and Nadia screeching. I was such a fool. He had a fucking wife he clearly still loved. *What is wrong with me?*

"Come on, Andi. It's time for lunch," Pepper grumbled, handing me my purse and grabbing my hand. Bray was trying to hide his anger with Jackson but his clenching jaw let me know that he was about to go off on him. I allowed Pepper to drag me out of the office and away from it all. The darkness was once again trying to creep back into my soul.

THE NOT-SO-DARK DAYS...

"He cried. Like a baby," I confide to Dr. Sweeney, picking at the frayed edge of the sofa cushion.

"Why do you think he cried?" he asks me, his eyes flickering to the cushion I was further destroying but not saying a word about it.

"I don't know. We'd only been out three times. That's the rule. Three dates and you're gone. It's not that hard really."

He writes something down into the notebook. I hate when he does that. It means I've said something wrong. Dammit.

"Do you have sexual relations on these dates?" he inquires, looking up from the notebook. Here it is—the moment I've been dreading.

"Yes," I whisper, glancing back down at the cushion.

"I see," is his reply and I can't help but hear the disappointment in his voice. Tears filled my eyes.

"I'm sorry, Dr. Sweeney. It started as dates but then I felt like I could forget about Bray and everything that we lost by fu...— having sex with these guys. I really think it's helping me. Dr. Sweeney, I swear it."

He shakes his head and writes something else down before setting the notebook aside. He grabs a tissue from the box on his desk and hands it to me. "Andi, you can't possibly think that being promiscuous is a solution to your depression from Brayden's infidelity, do you? I can't tell you what to do, but you remind me of my daughters. If you were my daughter, I would want someone to tell her that this isn't the way towards happiness. I know you say you're happy, but I don't think you truly are."

Damn Dr. Sweeney and his ultimate wisdom. Now I'm sobbing because I'm not happy. Sleeping around puts little band-aids on my bleeding wound, but they eventually fall. Thus, the need for a new one.

"I start my new job on Monday. I'm ready to put my life back in order, Dr. Sweeney. This is a promise to myself that, starting next week, things are going to be different." At least I will allow myself one more little band-aid before putting things on the right track.

"I have faith in you, Andi. You've come leaps and bounds. You are stronger than this depression. Keep telling yourself that and you'll be okay. See you next week. And I expect a full report on your exciting new job."

Chapter TWENTY-THREE

My sandwich sat untouched as Pepper fired off a text to someone. I couldn't eat. The thought of eating made me want to throw up. Jackson had been making out with his very naked wife in his office. It made me feel dirty and used, like I was the whore on the side. Those two had not looked like people who were in the middle of a nasty divorce.

I tore bits of my sandwich off and put them on the other side of the plate as I quietly thought about how sick I was. Sick of games. Sick of cheating. Sick of men. I was really going to make Dr. Sweeney work hard for his money tomorrow.

"I know what you're doing. You're playing with your food so it looks like you ate it. Andi, I've dealt with this before with you. If you don't eat your damn sandwich, I will shove it down your throat. We *are not* going through that again."

My eyes flew to hers. Her teary expression matched my own, but there was a determination in her eyes that made me pick up the sandwich and take a bite. The satisfied smile she gave me had me taking another bite.

After I had eaten most of the sandwich successfully without throwing it all up, she spoke again.

"I don't know what was going on with Nadia and Jackson, but it looked really shitty. I'm so sorry you had to see it. And as much as I hate to say this, maybe you should hear what he has to say. Blocking out Bray after what happened didn't help things out at all. At least even if Jackson tells you he's getting back with Nadia, you'll be able to move on. Promise me you'll talk with him."

I frown but nod because she's right. The last five months had been pure hell after what had happened with Bray. I couldn't allow myself to easily slip back into a depression.

We tossed our trash into the bin and headed outside so I could get back to work. The restaurant we had eaten at was close to my work, so the walk back was a quick one.

When we finally made it back to my desk, I noticed that Jackson's door was open and the light was off. He'd obviously gone home for the day.

Pulling me in for a hug, Pepper whispered, "You're going to be okay. I'm going to go in there and deal with dipshit Jordan. I'll see you at the apartment later. We're getting shitfaced tonight, Miss Andi."

I laughed as she pulled away and her eyes twinkled with relief. She was watching for signs of a relapse but I was stronger this time.

Sitting back down at my desk, I returned a few phone calls and caught up on some paperwork. Jackson never called or emailed or even showed back up. He was probably fucking Nadia right this moment. The rest of the day was torture as I counted down to quitting time.

Pepper had already stormed out of Jordan's office hours ago, and Bray stayed buried in paperwork. Olive texted me to tell me she'd be out late working on another photo shoot on the other side of the city.

When five finally rolled around, I gathered my things quickly so I could leave. Then Bray stopped in front of my desk.

"Come on. I'll make sure you get home okay."

I looked up at him, seeing concern written all over his face. "Bray, I can manage. I'm fine, really."

"It wasn't a question, Andi. Come on. Let's go."

Shaking my head at his bossiness, I stood and walked out with him. The ride in the cab back to my apartment was a quiet one. Pepper wouldn't be home from work until closer to six, so I let Bray in. He took a seat on the couch, looking around to take in everything that made this apartment our home.

"Want a drink, Bray?" I offered. He nodded, so I slipped into the kitchen and poured us each a glass of our favorite red wine. After today, I needed a drink. Chugging half of my glass, I quickly refilled it before heading back into the living room. He had moved across the room to look at some of the photographs I had taken.

"Andi, did you take these? They're amazing," he admired, sounding astonished. I felt a little embarrassed because they were more or less my secret little hobby that I used to get over him in the first place.

"Thanks. Here's your wine."

"So you want to talk about what happened today with Jackson?" he came right out and asked.

I chugged half my glass again before I spoke. "Not really, but I guess you're going to make me anyway, huh? Do you and Pepper have 'let's help Andi' talks? For as much as you guys hate each other, it sure seems like you both are on the same team."

I walked back into the kitchen, this time grabbing the bottle and bringing it back to the living room with me. I plopped down in the middle of the couch and refilled my glass. Bray made his way back over, sitting beside me.

"Have you talked to him?" Bray questioned, sipping his wine.

I shook my head and quickly drank more wine hoping it would start to take affect soon.

"No. He hasn't tried to contact me, which means he doesn't

want to. Clearly he wants to be with Nadia." I blinked back tears because it fucking hurt.

Bray patted my knee but left his hand there. I didn't make any moves to pull it away. Instead, I drained the rest of my glass and chuckled darkly as the numbness trickled through my body.

He took his hand from my leg and grabbed my glass, refilling it for me. His hand slipped back to my leg, but this time he placed it higher on my thigh.

Feeling his touch comforted me on some level. It wasn't that he turned me on—it just made me feel better.

"You know, Andi, you're going to be okay. Look how far you've come after what happened this past spring. This is just a blip compared to that."

It didn't feel like a blip. Jackson was more than just a blip to me. And just because I wasn't allowing the darkness to take over my soul again, didn't mean that it was any easier to handle.

When I sighed shakily, a tear slipped out and splashed on my thigh. Bray slid his thumb higher up my thigh to wipe it away. The gentle yet intimate touch mixed with the alcohol sent confusing messages through my body.

I looked over at him and his own eyes burned with need. Not taking time to think about if this was a good idea or not, I flung my leg over him and straddled him in one swift move. I could feel his hard cock through the silk of my panties and the soft materials of his slacks.

Our lips crashed onto one another's and I ground myself into him making him, making him moan from the contact. His hands jerked my skirt up my hips and slipped down into my panties, cupping my ass cheeks. We continued to kiss furiously. One of his hands moved around to the front and up under my camisole and jacket, finding my breast.

Gasping, I threw my head back out and shouted, "Jackson!"

Bray froze and pulled his lips away from my neck.

"Shit! I'm sorry Bray. Oh my gosh, I am so sorry." I started crying because this was wrong.

"Shh, Andi, it's okay. I don't feel right about this. We were kissing but you weren't there with me. You're still thinking about him because that's where you would rather be. I've lost you forever, but I'm okay with that. You need to talk to him. I just want you to be happy."

He removed his hand from underneath my shirt and the other from under my panties and used them to pull my skirt down some, even though I could still feel my ass sticking out. I leaned forward against his chest, burying my face, and sobbed. His hands wrapped around me and held me while I cried.

When the door opened, we both jerked our heads towards it. Jackson stood there with a shocked look on his face that was quickly masked by indifference. "Fucking unreal," he muttered as he walked right back out, slamming the door behind him.

I was sure to him it had looked way worse than it truly was. "Shit, Brayden, this is so bad!" I screeched, scrambling off of him. I yanked my skirt down and ran out the front door after him, shoeless.

When I made it downstairs, he was storming his way to his car. "Jackson, wait! It wasn't what it looked like," I cried out after him. He shook his head and dropped into the car, shutting the door. The car drove away, leaving me there to sob, barefoot on the street.

Chapter TWENTY-FOUR

"This is so messed up," I told her as she stroked my hair. Brayden had left once Pepper arrived. They appeared to be tag-teaming me today. I had just finished telling her all the crap that happened and was letting her soothe me with my head in her lap.

"You're right. It's completely messed up, Andi, but this is life. You have to learn to deal with these situations. When he cools off, talk to him. He owes you an explanation for the same fucking thing this morning."

I didn't say anything. I knew she was right. He had been quick to get pissed for the same thing. We needed to talk.

"The one good thing about it all was that you and Bray were finally able to put the idea of a possible reunion away. I think you both know that won't ever happen again."

I smiled because it was true. We were better off as friends. Even though we had once had a good connection, the heat I felt when I was with Jackson overpowered anything I had ever had with Bray. Dr. Sweeney would be proud at least of the healing that had taken place between me and Bray. He always said that I needed to forgive him. Bray would always hold a special place in my heart, but we could never become romantically involved again.

"Yeah, he says it's like kissing his sister now." I laughed at our earlier conversation.

"Gross, has he kissed his sister before? Shit, it's like he's got something to compare it to," she teased, trying to sound appalled. She knows he's an only child which doesn't make it any less funny.

We burst into giggles as Olive walked in. She took one look at us on the couch and ran over to sit with us, pulling my legs into her lap. These girls were like my sisters. They were always there when I needed them.

The next morning, I dressed with purpose. I was going to figure out a way to win Jackson back. He needed to see that Nadia was no good for him and that I was. We had something hot and meaningful together. I didn't want to throw it all away because of misunderstandings. I hoped that was really all that had been with him and Nadia.

Instead of a suit, I opted for a tight sweater dress. It was low cut, showing off my ample cleavage. It was shorter than my skirts, but I paired it with some heeled knee-high boots, attempting to not make it appear so short. Today, I was leaving the panties at home.

I made sure to straighten my hair, making my blond locks seem impossibly longer. My makeup looked sexy and dramatic. Glancing at my reflection, I smiled. I looked hot, and Jackson was going to notice. He always did.

My appointment with Dr. Sweeney wasn't until ten. That gave me some time to seduce Jackson.

Once I arrived, I strode right into his office, closing the door behind me. He looked up from his paperwork and his chocolate eyes darkened when he took in my appearance. Forcefully tearing his eyes away from me, he stared back down at his papers.

"Can I, uh, help you?" he stammered, hoarsely.

I sauntered over and around to his side of the desk and perched on the edge of it. His hands gripped both sides of his chair, knuckles turning white as he tried to refrain from touching me.

"Bray was comforting me. For a confused moment, I thought I wanted his touch, but it was only because I was trying to cover up the hurt you had caused me. I even called him Jackson." He smirked at that statement. "How do you explain what was going on with you and Nadia?"

"Nadia came in here trying to talk me out of the divorce. She's a money-hungry bitch. When she came in, she dropped her coat and threw herself at me. I was trying to push her away when you walked in. After you left, I completely bitched her out. I had to go after that because I needed to completely cool off before I talked to you."

He no longer could control his hand, and it slipped up to rest on my knee just above my boot. When I shivered from his touch, his eyes flew to mine, searing them with the heat in his gaze. I licked my lips, and his grip on my knee tightened, bruising the flesh. The space between my legs moistened as I anticipated more from him.

"Andi, things are nothing but complicated for us. I don't see how this could possibly work."

I spread my legs a little, giving him a preview, and he groaned. The bulge in his slacks was proof that he wanted me.

Ignoring his words, I slipped off the desk and knelt before him. His eyes melted me with their heat. Quickly, I unfastened his pants and yanked them down to his ankles. Looking up at him with hooded eyes, I licked the top of his shaft. His eyes rolled back in his head.

"Shit, Andi."

Taking those words as encouragement, I wrapped my mouth

around his large girth and began bobbing up and down. His hands found their way to my hair and he gripped tightly. I dug my fingernails into his thighs as I took him deep in my throat.

He cursed and pushed my head farther down, almost gagging me. But I relaxed as he pumped his orgasm down my throat. Pulling away, I licked the remaining semen off of my lips and his dick that had been falling flaccid jerked back to life. He really couldn't resist my lip licking.

He was looking down at me, his face unguarded and full of love. I beamed back at him, mirroring his face. His look quickly turned dark as he stood up, nearly knocking me over as he yanked his pants up and fastened them. "Get the fuck out of my office. Keep whoring around and you'll get your ass fired."

He was glaring down at me, and I suddenly felt like a fool. What was wrong with him? Tears rolled down my eyes as I awkwardly rose to my feet. His gaze softened for a split second but was fleetingly masked by one of hatred towards me.

Who was I kidding? This man harbored secrets that wouldn't allow him to get close to anyone. He'd proven it time and time again. My heart was going to fucking hurt after this one but he wouldn't break me. Been there. Done that. Not doing it again.

Straightening my skirt, I met his stare evenly. "You're going to die a lonely old man if you keep letting your shriveled-up black heart control your destiny. This was your last chance. I am worth more than what you clearly think I am. Have fun finding a new assistant, because I quit. I would suggest you hire a man. I'll send Jordan my formal resignation later this afternoon."

Turning on my heels, I stalked out of his office and towards Dr. Sweeney's.

"Andi, I've missed you. How are you doing?" Dr. Sweeney

asked once I settled onto the sofa in his office.

"I'm fine. It's been a hell of a week and you wouldn't believe me even if I tried to explain it," I sighed heavily.

"Try me," he quipped.

"Okay, so I had one more rendezvous last weekend and met a guy that I really liked. When I walked into my new job on Monday, he turned out to be my new boss. We tried to keep the relationship going, but he is so hot and cold with his emotions that it was really a battle. If things weren't awkward enough, Brayden started working there on Tuesday."

Dr. Sweeney eyed me over his glasses in disbelief. Glancing back down, he started writing in his damn notebook. Well, hell.

"Anyway, our budding relationship had me feeling alive for the first time since breaking up with Bray. I felt something in my little broken heart that made me realize it was still alive and ticking in there. And just as easily as he helped pump life into it, he wounded it as well. We've been playing a game of 'break it then fix it' over and over again."

He nodded at me, motioning for me to continue.

"We finally got to a good point in our relationship where he opened up some to me. Things were really looking up. That's until his ex showed up. I walked in his office and saw her naked body pressed against him. He appeared to be kissing her back and I was hurt. When I came back from lunch, he was gone. He never tried to call me or anything, leaving me to believe he had chosen her over me."

A tear slipped out even though I was angry over everything.

"Well, Brayden and I had kind of mended our relationship, happy to be just friends. He took me home and one thing led to another and we kissed." I left out the details because the frown on his face already told me he didn't like where this was going.

"Once Bray and I realized we were better as friends and that the kiss was a mistake, we hugged. Well Mr. Sometimes Hot and Sometimes Cold decided to walk in during that moment. I'm not going to lie, it looked pretty bad even though it wasn't. He stormed off and left me."

Dr. Sweeney continued to write in the notebook. At this rate, he'd have enough material for a novel. I wondered if he would use my real name or give me an alias. Maybe Jennifer Lawrence would play me in the movie. He cleared his throat, pulling me from my thoughts.

"This morning I decided I would get him back. I went into his office, and just when I thought we would be able to fix things for good, he turned back into his cold self, pushing me away for the final time. I told him I quit. So now I'm officially unemployed too."

His jaw dropped as he tried to find words to say but was interrupted when his secretary peeked her head in the door.

"I'm so sorry Dr. Sweeney, but one of your patients is here demanding to see you. He says it's an emergency."

"Carla, tell him I'll be right there."

She scurried back out of the office to pass on the message.

"Andi, I am so sorry. Sit tight while I go deal with this. I'm going to calm him down and reschedule him for after your appointment. He can wait twenty more minutes." He excused himself and stepped out of the office.

Hopefully Pepper will feel like going out tonight. I needed to force my mind to think about something other than the drama of Jackson.

Suddenly I heard shouting on the other side of the door. I scampered over to it to eavesdrop.

"I fucked up, Doc. She's gone for good. The one fucking thing I did right was get her to care for me but I went off and ruined it. I'm falling for her, Doc, but it's too late. You should have seen the look of horror on her face when I dismissed her. I fucking died inside but was too much of a coward to do anything about it."

Holy shit. The crazy patient was Jackson. I didn't even feel guilty a bit at eavesdropping because he was pouring out his heart about me. It was something he hadn't been able to do with me but my heart swelled at his words. He truly did care for me. It was all an act to protect his own heart.

"When I caught my own father fucking my wife in our bed, I *fucking* lost it. I vowed I would never open up to anyone again. Two people that I loved *the fucking most* had betrayed me. When this girl came along, she rocked my damn world. Everything I had trained myself to believe, she tested. She was changing me and it pissed me off. I don't deserve to be with someone like her. I'm a fucking murderer!"

What the hell? He was making absolutely no sense. Dr. Sweeney was talking in calm tones so I couldn't make out what he was saying back to Jackson. A murderer?

"I did murder him! I might not have pulled the trigger but it was because of me. If you had only heard the slew of terrible things I said to him, you would know that I forced him to believe those things that made him kill himself. I fucking hate him for sleeping with my wife. I fucking hate Nadia for sleeping with my father. I fucking hate him for taking his life. I fucking hate myself for being so damn stupid. What do I do, Doc? How do I get out of my own fucking head so that I can be happy for once in my miserable life?"

Wow. Jackson had said more stuff in the last five minutes than the entire time I had known him. After hearing him pour his guts out, I realized that he had only been pushing me away because I had been able to put a chink in his armor. He was protecting himself. Too bad for him, I'm a persistent bitch.

I opened the door and Jackson's jaw dropped when he saw me standing there. "You don't have to get out of your head. You just have to let me in," I explained, smiling hesitantly. His armor dropped, and I saw the vulnerable soul that had briefly showed itself over the course of our time together.

Decision passed over his face and he strode over to me, pulling me into his arms. His lips met mine and he kissed me tenderly. I snaked my arms around his neck. Our kiss would have lasted longer but the clearing of Dr. Sweeney's throat snapped us out of our trance.

"Come in the office. The three of us have discussing to do," Dr. Sweeney groaned as he shook his head, walking past us.

Jackson grabbed my hand, pulling me with him. We sat side by side on the sofa, hands locked together.

"You both are dealing with some things in your life that make you fragile and vulnerable. The two of you can either be a tremendous healer to the other or a knife in the wound. It is critical that you choose to be healers."

We both nodded and Jackson squeezed my hand.

"Your homework—" Dr. Sweeney began.

I groaned while Jackson muttered, "I hate this fucking shit."

Dr. Sweeney continued, ignoring Jackson's comment, "Your homework is to find things you both have in common besides sex. I want you guys to discover something you can do together. Jackson, I want you to work on telling Andi new things about yourself. Even things as inconsequential as your favorite color or stories from your childhood will help her develop trust in you. Andi, I want you to continue to build a friendship with Bray that is a healthy one. This will mean effort on your part, Jackson, to befriend him as well. Andi, I also want you to be open with Jackson and let him know when you feel like he's putting distance between the two of you. Together, you guys can make this work, but it will take a lot of effort on both your parts. You guys have had your hearts torn from your chests and are still surviving. Now get out of here. I'll see you both together same time next week. I'm going to lunch."

With that, he stood and left us holding hands on the couch.

"I'm sorry for being such an ass," he apologized, his free hand cupping my cheek.

"I forgive you," I winked.

He jumped away from me and strode over to the door, turning

the lock. The grin he gave me was one of his mischievous, boyish ones.

"I should have done this when you came into my office this morning." He walked over to me and gently pushed me down onto the couch. His hands slid up my thighs and under my dress to my hips. I arched my back at his sensual touch. He growled when he became aware of my lack of panties.

I laughed at his animalistic sound but quickly cried out when his mouth devoured my wet pussy. My bodily involuntarily bucked against his mouth as he licked and sucked furiously between my folds. I came quickly this way and shuddered as my orgasm shocked its way through my body. When I finally relaxed, he pulled away, chuckling.

"Is it safe to say I drive you just as crazy as you drive me?" he asked.

"You just gave me oral sex in our shrink's office. I think it's safe to assume we're on the same level of crazy."

"Well, babe, things are about to get a little more crazy because I'm not finished with you." We christened the Dr. Sweeney's couch and it was fucking amazing.

JACKSON'S DARK DAYS...

Nadia has been so distant lately. I know she wants a baby, but damn, we don't have time for it. Jordan and I are trying to learn the ropes of Dad's company. Dad's been so fucking insistent lately that we learn all of the ins and outs. He's been working us to the bone. My relationship with Nadia has suffered because of it.

I was supposed to be meeting with one of Dad's big clients. He was having dinner with Mom tonight, so he asked me to handle it for him. When the client rescheduled, I decided to take opportunity to surprise Nadia. I already made reservations to the fanciest restaurant in town. I just have to go pick her up so we can get there by seven.

She's going to be surprised to see me home so early. I'm really making an effort to work on our relationship. In fact, tonight I'm going to tell her that we should try for a baby. We'll start tonight. Hell, we might start before dinner.

When I step into our loft, I hear her soft voice in the bedroom. It sounds like she is pleasuring herself with her vibrator. I'm ashamed at how much she's had to use the damn thing because of my work schedule. Her moans have my dick hardening in my pants. Whatever little fantasy she's having right now will soon be interrupted.

Before I enter the room, I rip off my jacket and shirt. Walking in, I start unbuttoning my pants. "Babe, let's make a fucking baby," I say smugly, looking up for her reaction.

Seconds tick by as I take in the scene. My wife is being plowed by some asshole. She screams when she sees me standing there. Running over to them, I rip him off of her and punch him in the face. I punch my father in his face. Fuck. MY. FUCKING. FATHER.

Chapter TWENTY-FIVE

"Is Jordan pissed that we both took today off?" I asked Jackson as I knelt to tie my shoelace.

He bent over, touching his toes to stretch. My eyes raked across his ass in his wind pants. His shirt was stretched across his muscled chest and I had a hard time focusing when he replied.

"Nah, I told him we had homework to do. He was a little preoccupied. I think he really has a thing for Pepper. Too bad she won't give him the time of day. It's fucking hilarious if you ask me."

I laughed because Pepper doesn't give anyone the time of day. We decided to try running as something we could do together. Running was something I used to do before Bray and I broke up. Jackson said that he'd been too busy for working out lately, so this was a win-win for us.

We ran for a good three miles before we made our way back to Jackson's loft. He kept trying to rub his sweat on me and I was about to deck him. Finally having had enough, I tickled him on his sides, making him go crazy. Before he had time to respond, I took off up the stairs not wanting him to catch me on the elevator. I was halfway up the first flight of stairs when I heard the door burst open below me.

"You are so going to get it!" he boomed from the bottom of the stairwell. Squealing, I picked up the pace taking the steps two at a time. I could hear his shoes slapping the stairs as he raced to catch up with me.

"Fat chance, Jackie!" I taunted him as I tore up the stairs. I had to be at least two flights above him now. Just as I was rounding the curve to go up the next flight, hands roughly grabbed my waist and pulled me backwards.

"No!" I shrieked. Dammit, he had caught up to me! His hand seized the top of my yoga pants and roughly pulled them down, baring my ass. His other hand jerked his wind pants down. He bent me over and shoved himself between my legs.

"Oh God, Jackson!" I moaned as he slammed into me wildly.

One of his hands made it up to my breast and tweaked the nipple through the material of the sports bra. Fucking in a stairwell was incredibly naughty.

"Fuck, baby, I'm there!" I cried out as my climax ripped through me. I was still clenching with the aftershocks when I felt his orgasm pump into me.

He pulled out, still dripping, and quickly yanked his pants back up. His hand popped my ass and I squealed. I snatched my yoga pants back up into place just as the door opened and a security guard walked in.

"Ma'am, is everything okay? We got some complaints of a woman screaming in the stairwell," he informed, his eyes darting over to Jackson.

My face burned with embarrassment. "Uh, yes, everything is fine. We were just horsing around. I'm so sorry. We'll be quieter."

He looked between us and nodded. Jackson grabbed my hand and we bolted up the last few levels. When we made it safely into his loft, I punched him in his gut.

"You're such an ass! What if that guy had seen us having sex?" I exclaimed.

Jackson laughed as he headed towards his bathroom. "It would have given him something to spank off to later."

"Gross, Jackson! You're so crude. That is so something Pepper would say." He was naked by the time he reached the shower, and I admired his nice ass as he slipped into it. I peeled off my sweaty clothes and joined him inside.

He stepped aside so we both could stand under the steady stream of hot water. I wrapped my hands around his waist and rested my cheek on his chest. His hands came around to rest just above my butt.

"That was fun, Andi. Running is definitely something we can do together. And contrary to Doc's beliefs, the sex afterwards was pretty therapeutic."

I giggled into his chest and he rubbed his hands up my back. "You're impossible, Jackie." That comment garnered a slap to my ass.

JACKSON'S DARK DAYS...

The past few days have been hell. Dad begged me not to say anything to Jordan or Mom. I couldn't even speak to him without wanting to punch him in the fucking face. All Jordan knows is that I caught Nadia sleeping with another man. He is letting me crash at his place until she moves all of her things to her mother's house. Dad asked me to come to his house to talk about some things since Mom would be away at church.

I reluctantly agreed at the time, so here I am standing on the porch, waiting for him to answer the door. He calls for me to come in, so I walk inside. Knowing he'll probably be in his office, I head over to it.

His appearance is haggard. The hair on his head is disheveled, and his jawline is getting scruffy as well. The half-empty bottle of Wild Turkey sits proud on his desk.

"Hey, son." The room reeks of liquor.

"What do you want from me, Dad?" I ask, still standing in the doorway.

"Son, I am so damn sorry. Recently, things haven't been going the way I want them too. I lost my head and did some stupid things. Please forgive me."

My jaw clenches. This is fucking ridiculous. I can't even look him in the eye.

Storming into the office, I slam both fists down on the desk, making the bottle wobble.

"You fucking slept with my wife, Dad. Do you know how fucking sick you are to do that to me? We were going to try for a baby!"

"Dammit, Jackie! I said I'm sorry. Your wife came on to me by the way. I'm just an old man. When Nadia came on to me, I lost my head. I needed to feel powerful and on top of the world again. Just for a while, it made me feel that way." He rubbed his face

165

with his hands.

"Dad, I am so over talking about this. Do you know how hard it is not to tell Jordan or Mom? You cheated on my mother with my wife! This is fucking with my mind, Dad."

"Son, please. I just need to hear that you forgive me. It's the only thing that matters to me right now." Opening his desk drawer, he pulls out his revolver and sets it on the desk in front of him.

My hands go into defense mode when I see the gun.

"Dad, calm down. Shit, put the gun away. Nobody needs to get hurt."

He picks it up and I flinch.

"I need to hear it, Jackie."

"Fuck, Dad! I forgive you, okay? Can you put the gun away now?"

"I love you, Jackie." Raising the gun, he slips it into his mouth and pulls the trigger, blowing his brains all over the blinds behind him. I love you too, Dad.

Chapter TWENTY-SIX

Jackson was taking me out on a date tonight. He said that he wanted to take me to a new sushi restaurant that already was getting rave reviews. Of course I agreed. Dr. Sweeney would be proud that we can do other things besides have sex.

When I turned off the hair dryer, I heard shouts in the other room. Setting it on the counter, I padded barefoot into Jackson's living room.

The air was punched out of my gut when I saw Bitch Nadia reaching out for Jackson.

"Jackie, please don't make me sign these papers. We can work it out," she begged him.

"Nadia, no. Get the fuck out of my house. I can't look at you. Sign the fucking papers and let me live my life without you poisoning it."

She walked up to him and cupped him between the legs. Before he even had an opportunity to push her away, I tore across the living room toward her, seeing red the entire way.

I tackled her to the ground and started hitting her with my

fists. Her hands found my hair and tried to yank me off of her. I clawed at her hands and she howled when I drew blood.

Strong arms hooked under me and yanked me off of her. I tried to fight him off to get back to her but he held me tight.

"You bitch! You're a home-wrecking whore!" I screamed down at her.

Nadia scrambled to her feet. She looked rumpled and frazzled, no longer the poised woman who was standing here moments ago.

"Call your dog off, Jackie! You're the home wrecker. You're sleeping with MY husband!" she spat.

I tried to get back over to her but Jackson held me tight.

"Nadia, it's time for you to leave. You aren't welcome here. Nothing you say or do will make me change my mind. Now go before I call building security."

Throwing one more bitchy look my way, she snatched up her purse and stalked out, slamming the door behind her.

"I am so sorry about that. She is one of the skeletons in my closet that won't fucking go away." He squeezed me from behind.

My chest still heaved from our altercation.

"You are so hot when you're pissed," he whispered into my hair. His hands slipped under my dress and caressed circles on the outsides of my thighs. And just like always, I melted at his touch.

I was pretty sure he was going to bend me over and fuck me over the back of the couch again. Instead, he surprised me by scooping me up into his arms. He carried me to his bedroom and sat me down on the bed. Ripping off his t-shirt, he revealed his muscled chest, making me want him immediately. He unbuckled his jeans, letting them fall to the floor. His boxers followed not long after. My eyes fell to his cock that was hard and at attention.

Grabbing the hem of my dress, I pulled it up over my head and tossed it to him. He laughed at my playfulness but quickly growled once he realized I had had nothing on under the dress.

"Damn, woman," he groaned with pleasure, crawling over me, kissing my neck. His kisses sprinkled my neck, breasts, and abdomen.

When he looked up at me with those brown eyes, I nearly lost it. "Make love to me."

Nodding, he positioned himself at my entrance and slid into my already wet core. His lips met mine and our tongues danced with their own melody. The thrusts were slow and deliberate, making my orgasm tease just out of reach. He sucked my lip into his mouth and I moaned loudly.

"You're so beautiful like this," he admired as he pressed his forehead to mine.

His thrusts quickened as did the nearing of my climax. It crashed over me and my body shook from the intensity. My eyes fluttered shut, and I felt his release moments later.

When I opened my eyes again, he was watching me with such intensity. I grinned up at him.

"Andi, I fucking love you." There was no trace of humor or teasing. His fragile soul was reflected in those chocolate brown eyes. I loved seeing this side of him.

"I fucking love you too."

JACKSON'S DARK DAYS...

"No!" Jordan yells at me through the phone. I'm crying like a fucking baby. I can't look over at his body slumped over his desk, brains splattered all over the curtains.

"Jordie, shit! I fucking watched him put a gun in his mouth and pull the trigger. He's dead, Jordie." I sob into the phone.

"Mom..." He trailed off. We both are sniffling into the phone, silently worrying about how this would affect her.

"Man, I need you here. I'm about to fucking lose it. The cops are on the way but I need my brother."

"I can't see him like that," he whispers into the phone.

My eyes skirt over to my dad's body and I quickly look away.

"You don't have to. I just need you. We need to get strong before Mom comes home. Please, Jordie. Hurry."

"Was it Dad?" he questions. I know what he means. He wants to know if it was Dad who slept with Nadia.

"Yeah, man. I caught them in the act. It was fucking sick."

"That's fucked up, Jackson. I'm so sorry. Sit tight, I'm on my way."

Chapter
TWENTY-SEVEN

The restaurant was swanky and modern. We'd just finished our delicious dinner and were sipping on some sake, enjoying our date. This sushi restaurant was a new favorite for sure. It was terribly expensive but definitely worth it.

Jackson looked sexy as always, his dark hair styled perfectly on his head. His tight shirt that stretched across his sculpted chest did crazy things to my insides. From under his dark lashes, his chocolate eyes met mine. The intensity in his eyes assured me that I did similar things to his insides as well.

"So what was your thing? Dr. Sweeney made me find a hobby to help get over Bray. What hobby did you find?" I asked him.

His eyes darkened. I could tell that he didn't want to tell me but was going to anyway. He sighed and cleared his throat.

"I really don't want to tell you because it's kind of embarrassing."

My curiosity was about to kill me. I absolutely needed to know what he did.

"Tell me, Jackson! You promised you would open up."

He sighed once again, really stalling. His eyes darted to mine, his face completely serious.

"Do you know all those times I shut my office door?" he questioned, still stalling.

Creepy porn habit? Whatever his hobby was, we could deal with it together.

"Go on, Jackson. Tell me. Don't be embarrassed. It's just me."

He palmed his face and then pinned me down with his hard stare. Shit. This was bad whatever it was. I braced myself. Whatever it was, I didn't care. He was my man and I loved him.

"I am an administrator on a website…" He trailed off, hesitating again.

My sweet Jackson was running a porn site. Damn.

He continued his explanation. "I'm an administrator for a Harry Potter fan club site," he huffed out finally.

Come again?

"Wait, what?"

"Andi, those books are amazing. On our site, we do podcasts, post hilarious memes, point out mistakes in the movies that don't match up with the books…"

He was still talking but I completely tuned him out. Big bad Jackson was a Harry Potter nerd. The gleam in his eyes while nervously spouting off all that he does for the site was boyish and adorable, making my heart swell with pride. The excitement in his voice made me break into a huge grin.

"Jackson," I said, cutting him off. "Dare I say I've never read the books? I watched one movie and fell asleep." I knew this would egg him on but it was so worth it.

His face was full of shock, like I had just insulted his mother. Tossing a handful of cash on the table, he scooted out of the booth and snatched my hand, pulling me out. He hurriedly dragged me from the restaurant.

Once outside, I finally protested.

"Hey! Where are we going?" I asked, laughing at his

demeanor.

"The bookstore. I cannot allow my woman to be uneducated on all things Harry Potter. If we have any hope for this relationship surviving, you are going to read those damn books," he grinned at me. I laughed the entire way to the bookstore.

Jackson stacked the books on the counter at the register. He reminded me of a little boy like this. It was incredibly adorable. Discovering new things about him made me so happy, even the completely random and unusual things.

"Did you find everything okay?" the cashier inquired.

He practically growled at her and she flinched. *Damn, Jackson. Chill, dude.*

"No. How can you not have Harry Potter and the Goblet of Fire? One of the most popular series in the world and you run out of the fourth book. Who's in charge of ordering around here?" he demanded seriously. I burst out laughing at him and the cashier nervously looked at me, unsure what to think about us.

"Don't mind him. He's obsessed with Harry Potter. Once he figures out how slow I read, he'll soon realize we have plenty of time to order it online and have it shipped."

He was still upset about the book but didn't harass the poor woman anymore.

Once we got back out to the car with our loot, I teased him. "Sheesh, Jackson. What if I don't like your books? Are you going to break up with me?"

"You're going to love them. J.K. Rowling is a genius," he promised. He was so cute. Even if I hated the books, I'd never let him know. It was very much a part of him and I loved that. Harry and I were about to become best friends.

I opened the bag and peered in. Sure, we didn't have book

four, but we had the rest of them plus three supplemental books. He was going to be easy to buy for at Christmas. He pulled a book into his hand and was admiring it.

Sliding my hand up his thigh, I brought my mouth to his ear and nibbled. He tensed underneath me.

"I'm kind of jealous of this J.K. Rowling chick. You seem to be way more interested in her rather than me," I teased as I sucked his lobe between my teeth.

He gasped and I heard him toss the book. His hands pulled me into his lap, and one of them sneaked underneath my dress. I slid my legs on either side of him, giving his fingers free access. Two of them glided into me easily since I was still bare underneath my dress and I moaned. I hoped he had hit the button giving privacy between us and George.

I rode his hand as he finger-fucked me and it felt amazing. His other hand pulled the low neckline of my dress down, freeing my breasts. He leaned forward and sucked on a nipple. My pussy clenched around his fingers, which only encouraged him to thrust them harder into me.

My body convulsed as the orgasm crashed over me. His fingers remained inside of me as his thumb slid over my clit. I shuddered at the touch. He did insane things to my body. When he made me come once more, I sighed happily and threw my arms around his neck.

"You're the only thing I'm interested in. Everything else fails miserably short compared to you," he whispered to me.

Take that, J.K. Rowling.

JACKSON'S DARK DAYS...

"Richard? Why are the police here?" Mom frantically calls from the front door. Jordan and I stand from the sofa. When her face sees mine, she wails and collapses to the floor. I don't know how she knows, but she does. We run to her and the three of us sob. I'm clutching on to Mom, and Jordan has his arms around both of us.

"I need to see him," she shrieks, attempting to stand up. Jordan and I hold her still.

"No. Mom, you can't. I'm so sorry," I tell her sadly.

She begins cursing at us and clawing at me so I'll let go but I don't. Just like I wouldn't let Jordan see, I won't let my mother see. I wish I could take those horrible images from my mind and burn them away. There's no way my family will ever have to bear that scene in their memory banks.

She finally gives up on her hysterical attempt of escaping my arms and lets me hold her. "Boys, I am so sorry. So, so sorry."

Me too, Mom. Me too.

Chapter TWENTY-EIGHT

The morning sun seeped into my room and blanketed his hard sleeping body. He was quite beautiful, especially in such a peaceful form. I slid out of my bed, trying not to wake him. His soft breathing let me know that he was still blissfully asleep. I picked up my camera from the dresser and snapped the photo. From a few other angles, I captured the shots I wanted. It was like I had a dark-headed angel in my bed, and he was gorgeous.

When I climbed onto the bed to get a better angle, his eyes suddenly opened and his hand shot out and grabbed my thigh. He grinned at me, looking impossibly more beautiful. I took another picture of him.

"What kind of creepy person takes pictures of people sleeping?" he asked, laughing at me.

"I take pictures of beautiful things and you are one of those beautiful things."

Pulling the camera from me, he started taking pictures of me as I tried pulling the sheets over my naked body.

His eyes raked over my body, and when they met mine again,

they were smoldering. I gasped at his heated gaze, and he stole one more photo before setting the camera on the bedside table.

"You're a beautiful thing too, you know. Every day I am still shocked you're mine. Still amazed that you would pick me out of everyone. I'm broken but you want me anyway. That makes you perfect in my eyes," he revealed, lowering himself over my body and gently kissing my lips.

"Are you kidding me, Jackson? I'm broken too. That's what makes us perfect for each other. We understand each other's pain. It makes us stronger. I thank God every day for the way things happened, because if they hadn't, I would never have found you. When I look at you, Jackson, I can see into your soul. I hope when you look at me you can see into mine as well. You're all I ever wanted. You're all I'll ever want."

His vulnerable eyes met mine again and we stared into each other's souls in the way that was unique to us. He positioned himself at my folds and slid easily in. His eyes never left mine as he slowly pumped into me. This wasn't sex or making love. This was the joining of two broken souls, making one strong, perfect one.

When we finally came simultaneously together, a tear escaped my eye. He wiped it away with his thumb and kissed me softly on the lips again. "I love you, Andi."

This moment was one that I wished I could bottle up and save for a rainy day. "I love you too, Jackson."

"Will Jordan be there?" I asked Jackson as we pulled down his mother's street.

"He's supposed to, and so is Pepper," he answered, looking at me and we both laughed. It was still debatable if Pepper would be there or not. She hadn't seemed thrilled at the idea of having dinner with him and his family. Jordan was unstoppable when it came to her. I just hoped that he liked her as much as I thought he did. If she ever decided to crack her icy exterior, Jordan would be worth cracking it for.

George stopped the car and got out with us. Trish insisted that he join us for dinner. Quite honestly, I thought she was sweet on the adorable British man.

We walked inside and the smell of roast swirled around me, instantly making my stomach growl. Jackson laughed beside me and I elbowed him in the ribs.

"Come in, everyone! The roast is almost ready. Can I offer you all some wine?" Trish asked as she breezed around the kitchen.

We all accepted her offer and watched as she finished up the supper.

"Where's Jordie? Does he plan on coming? Is he bringing a date?" she inquired, her voice hopeful.

"I'm not sure, Mom. Last I heard, he planned on coming and he was going to bring Andi's roommate. You never know with him though."

She smiled and handed us our glasses. We sipped on them while Trish asked George if he wanted to go to church with her tomorrow. Jackson cocked an eyebrow at me over his wineglass and I grinned.

"Mom? Where's my favorite lady?" Jordan's voice boomed from the living room. Her face lit up as she ran from the kitchen. I loved how close this family was. It was such a far cry from my own. We walked into the living room to see Jordan hugging Trish.

"I'm still upset with you, Jordie. You haven't visited in weeks. Jackson definitely moved into first place for favorite son," she teased.

Jordan grinned at her, handing her a box of Godiva's chocolates. "Who's your favorite son now?" he asked as she shrieked, snatching the box from him. We all chuckled at them.

A knock on the front door grabbed our attention, and Jordan reached behind him, opening it. His smile was huge as he motioned for Pepper to come in. She frowned at him but broke into a smile when she saw me.

Jordan introduced them. "Mom, this is Andi's roommate, Pepper. Pepper, this is my mother, Trish." Pepper let out a yelp of surprise when Trish pulled her in for a hug. She'd learn that this was an affectionate family, especially Jordan and his mother.

"It's so nice to meet you, Pepper. You are such a lovely girl. Perfect for my Jordie," she praised as she let her go. Pepper started to protest but Trish interrupted her. "Roast is ready!"

Trish scampered into the kitchen, George following behind her.

"This is not a date!" she hissed at Jordan once Trish was out of earshot. He only grinned at her, further pissing her off.

Jackson and I tried to suppress our smiles but it was hard. There was so much sexual tension rolling off those two. Pepper needed to just get over it because I was absolutely positive she would enjoy herself once she did.

She glared over at us. "I've got somewhere to be in an hour so let's get this over with."

Stomping into the kitchen after Trish, she left the three of us to laugh after her.

Trish outdid herself once again. The roast was tender and amazing. When she brought out the chocolate cake, I almost died and went to heaven. It was fabulous. The dinner went surprisingly well, and even Pepper smiled a few times at Jordan's elaborate stories of him and Jackson as kids. When Trish offered everyone some coffee, Pepper stood.

"Thank you, Trish, for dinner. It was wonderful. I must get going now though. My dad is taking me to a movie later."

"Oh, hon, you're welcome. Please visit again. I love how full my kitchen is right now. We haven't had this many laughs in this house in quite some time."

Jordan got up to walk her to the front door. From my position, I could see them standing at the front door. They were arguing in hushed tones. Those two were impossible. Suddenly, Jordan took her cheeks into his hands and pulled her in for a passionate kiss. My jaw dropped as I elbowed Jackson, catching his attention.

The kiss lasted a few moments, and I could see Pepper melting in his grasp. But suddenly, her body tensed and she jerked away from him. Her hand flew towards him, slapping him hard across the cheek. Jackson and I gasped.

Jordan reached for her hand but she yanked it away, bolting out the front door. What the hell had just happened? Angrily, Jordan turned on his feet and stalked back into the kitchen.

"That girl is impossible," he huffed as he heaved himself back into his chair.

We all sat quietly for a moment before George changed the subject and started talking about the Elton John concert that was supposed to be coming to Central Park soon.

Jordan's jaw clenched and unclenched continuously. I couldn't believe Pepper was so against dating him. When I got home, I was going to drill her on why she was being so difficult.

JACKSON'S DARK DAYS...

"Your father was a part of some less than legal business dealings. There may even have been some shell companies involved. Now that he's passed on, one of the men he did some business with is demanding to know where his cut is. The man, Lou Jennings, is quite influential so we have to tread lightly with this. It won't sit well for him if we just ignore it. He wants to settle but it will be pricey. Two other smaller companies have also come forward with allegations against Compton Enterprises. They are all willing to avoid a lawsuit if you pay the money this company supposedly owes them. We can try and fight them all in court, but I fear it will just open up a huge can of worms this company can't afford to deal with," our company attorney Joel Dickson tell us.

Jordan is visibly pissed. He's lives and breathes this company, so this not only shocks him but it angers him as well. Dad just keeps fucking with us, even from the grave.

"So what you're telling us is that we need to pay out or potentially have our company ruined with lawsuits?" he growls at Joel.

Unfazed, Joel nods his head. "Yes, that's exactly what I'm saying. Unfortunately, Richard left you guys with a huge mess. I don't know what all exactly he was involved in, but this could potentially ruin the company if you don't cooperate. Mr. Jennings has a lot of money and could make your lives a living hell."

I rub my face with my hands. Finally, Jordan slams his pen down on the table. "Set up the meeting, Joel. We'll try to negotiate something with this asshole. I'm ready to fucking move on. This is our company now, and we run things differently."

Chapter TWENTY-NINE

Jackson had his laptop perched on the arm of the sofa as he answered messages on his site. My head rested in his lap while I read the first book in the series. It turned out to be better than the movie and I was having trouble putting it down. He brought a hand down to my hair and gently stroked it. This moment was serene and blissful.

When his phone rang, he dug it out of his pocket.

"Hey, Jordie. What's up?" he chirped.

Yelling could be heard through the phone. Jackson tensed and sat up. I lifted off of him and tried to hear what was going on that had him a bundle of nerves. He glanced at me and flew off of the couch and toward his bedroom, shutting the door behind him.

Whatever they were speaking about had him pissed. I could hear him yelling back at Jordan. My stomach did flip-flops because he had reverted back to Cold Jackson when he jumped from the couch. I could feel the knife in the wound Dr. Sweeney had spoken about. Blinking back some tears, I tried to read some more of my book.

Finally after a few quiet moments, I decided to check on Jackson. I opened the door and found him sitting on the bed, running his hand through his hair. It appeared he was still on the phone but was just listening to Jordan. I started backing away to give him privacy. His cold eyes met mine and he glared at me.

"What the fuck, Andi? I came in here to speak privately to Jordan. You're being a fucking snoop!" He stormed toward me and I backed away from him, hating the look in his eyes. The door slammed in my face and my heart.

Tears began falling down my face as I shakily grabbed my book and purse. I slipped out the front door and ran to the elevator. Once downstairs, I bolted down the street and hailed a cab. On the cab ride back to my apartment, I cried hysterically in the back seat. The cab driver, being from New York and having seen it all, didn't even flinch or look my way in concern.

Why was Jackson shutting me out again? I had thought we were past all of this. I knew his secrets now, so why in the hell was he doing this to me again?

Once I was back in my apartment, I sighed, relieved that Pepper and Olive weren't there. I wanted some time alone. Slipping into my bedroom, I set my stuff down and closed the door. I walked over to my bed and sat down.

Seeing my camera, I reached over and began scanning though the pictures. The first one was of me. My mouth was parted and my nipple peeked above the top of the sheet. I actually did look beautiful and happy there. A tear raced down my cheek. The next few were of me laughing. When I got to the next one, my stomach ached.

Jackson was looking at me, grinning. His barriers were down and he was mine in this picture. This was the Jackson I knew. Cold Jackson was an ass, but I missed him too. The next couple of pictures were of him sleeping, and he was amazingly beautiful. Why did he insist on pushing me away?

Fresh tears rolled down my cheeks. I was crying loudly when

my bedroom door burst open, revealing my beautiful, angry Jackson. He stormed over to me and pulled me from the bed into his arms.

"I'm so sorry, Andi. All I do is fuck up with you! Jordan snapped me out of the zone I was in by hanging up on me after I yelled at you. It all came crashing over me. I was such a jackass to you. This is why I don't deserve you. I mess up too much. When you were gone, my heart fucking shattered to bits. I can't live without you, Andi," he revealed, squeezing me to him.

I didn't answer him. I just continued to cry into his chest.

"I didn't mean to shut you out. I'm still learning here. The company is going through some serious shit right now. We might get sued by several different companies. If we don't settle particularly with this asshole, Lou Jennings, our company is in major jeopardy. He wants a ridiculous amount of money. If we give pay him what he feels he's owed, it will put us in a huge financial problem. It's a complicated mess and we're stressed to the max about it. I'm so, so sorry that I pushed you away instead of allowing you to be there with me for it."

His confession warmed my soul even though I felt bad about what he was going through. He did love me but still had a hard time opening up. We could work through this.

"I love you, Jackson. More than anything, I need you to be open with me. Don't shut me out. I want to be here for you through the good and the bad."

"God, Andi. I love you so much. Promise me you won't leave me again. Next time, just punch me in the gut because I'll deserve it."

"How about I make up for lost time?" I teased and punched him hard in the stomach. Must not have been too hard because his laughter boomed through the room. It was music to my ears.

I stood on my toes and kissed him, forgiving him once again. I'd always forgive this man. And as we fell to the bed in each other's arms, kissing wildly, we spent the rest of the afternoon making perfectly imperfect love.

Epilogue

Jackson—A few weeks later

"Andi, I have to show you something," I called to her from my office. She slipped into my office, closing the door behind her and locking it. Her sexy, long legs were shooting out from underneath her short suit skirt. My gaze skittered up her legs. Her perky breasts were peeking their tops out of her camisole under her jacket. My eyes landed there and I had trouble bringing them up to hers.

When they finally made it to her face, I see that she was grinning at me and my heart swelled. This funny, smart, gorgeous woman belonged to me. I smiled back at her and motioned her over.

"What is it, Mr. Compton? Make any new Harry Potter memes I need to see?" She was so fucking hot when she sassed me.

"Get over here, smartass," I growled at her.

She laughed and stood beside me, peering at my computer screen. Her laughter died when she read the email.

"Jackson! This is fantastic news!" she squealed, hopping into my lap. I'd just received the email from my attorney. My divorce was final.

She kissed me hard on my lips and suddenly I wanted to celebrate with my woman. I stood her up in front of me. Her heat-filled eyes met mine and she licked her lips. I fucking wanted to pounce on her every time she did that. My dick bulged against my pants.

Quickly, I spun her around and pushed her down across my desk. Her hands shoved some papers into the floor and I grinned as it reminded me of our first heated session together over Ian's desk. Long blond hair delicately fell around her. She was even more beautiful than the first time I fucked her like this.

Grabbing the bottom of her skirt, I hiked it up over her hips, revealing her pale, perfect ass. My dick throbbed once I realized she wasn't wearing panties today. She killed me when she did this. I spent half my day worrying if anyone would accidentally catch a peek and the other half of the day wanting to shove my dick in her. It made for difficult working conditions.

I slid one of my fingers into her body, and she moaned. She was always so wet and ready for me. I couldn't ever get enough of her. Knowing what she liked, I slapped her bottom with my free hand. She groaned in desire, pushing her ass closer to me. Luckily everyone, including Bray and Jordan, had gone home already.

Her white cheek was now turning a deep shade of pink and I was about to come in my pants because it turned me on so much. I slapped the spot again, this time harder like she likes it. She wailed in pleasure, "Yes! Jackson!"

Her ass was bright red at this point. Just when she was about to unravel from her orgasm, I pulled my finger out of her. She shuddered at the loss.

Jerking off my pants as fast as I could get them off, I admired her sexy body as it waited for me. This woman was it for me. My life was perfect with her in it.

Lining my cock up against her opening, I teased her as I barely dipped it in. "Jackson, please," she begged. Not being able to resist her, I slammed into her. I groaned and she cried out. Pumping in and out of her, I could feel myself about to lose control. Reaching around her, I rubbed her clit and helped her orgasm get here quickly since mine was about to erupt.

Her breaths were coming fast and ragged. She finally screamed my name as I felt her pussy clench deliciously around my dick, sending my own release burning through me.

We were fucking amazing together. What had started out as a weekend of fun turned into more than I could have ever imagined. I'd say she definitely won the game because I would be lost without her.

The End

Coming Soon…

Want more Pepper and Jordan? ***Wrong (Breaking the Rules #2) –
Coming early spring***

Want more Olive and Bray? ***Scarred (Breaking the Rules #3) –
Coming late spring/early summer***

Acknowledgements

This whole becoming an author thing has been quite the rollercoaster ride! All it took was one conversation from a childhood friend, Kim Easton, at a book signing to thrust me into the world of writing. Sure, I'd always had a knack for writing when it came to school assignments, but this was the first time I even attempted to do it in a fun, creative way. Once she lit the fire, I went wild. I'll be forever grateful that she lit the match and told me to "run!"

I also want to thank my beta readers, whom are also my friends. Leann Jester, Mandy Abel, Star Price, and Erica Thompson, you guys provided AMAZING support. Pointing out areas that didn't work and gushing over parts you loved, you helped boost the confidence I needed to finish what I'd started. I can't thank you enough and look forward to sending you more of my stories in the future.

While on this journey, I made some fabulous online friends (they aren't creepers, Mom) who've helped guide me along the way. I know I'll need to hop on a plane to Australia to see you, Maree Hunter, my "sister from another mother" and give you a big hug. When I found a lovely group of established authors on Facebook, I nearly peed my pants when they invited me to join their super-secret club! The Indie Romance Authors Corner showed me the ropes every step of the way. Love you girls! A huge thanks to my NKOTB bestie, Jacquelyn Ayres. I would have gotten a lot more sleep if I'd never have met you, but I would never have found someone just as dirty-minded as myself. It's nice sharing my "research" with you.

Robin at Wicked by Design, you totally rocked out an awesome cover for me that I can be proud of. You made the process seamless and easy, jumping over hoops to meet my frenzied deadlines. Mickey, my fabulous editor from I'm a Book Shark, without you, my story would have about 1,376 less commas and my characters would be grossly overusing the word "said". Thank you for not only, coming to my aide in a pinch and turning my story back to me so quickly that my head spun, but also for helping my novel be the best that it could be. Wendy Shatwell, head hauncho of Bare Naked Words, thanks for pimping my book and holding my hand all the way from the UK.

A huge thanks goes out to my wonderful husband, Matt. Without you, I wouldn't have been able to make this dream possible as it took a lot of time and money. Not only did you write check after check when I "needed" something else for my book, but you also kept the children fed and bathed. Tighten those apron straps because I don't have plans of stopping any time soon!

Lastly, thank you to all of the wonderful readers out there that are willing to hear my story and enjoy my characters like I do. It means the world to me!

About the Author

I'm a thirty two year old self-proclaimed book nerd. Married to my husband for nearly eleven years, we enjoy spending time with our two lovely children. Writing is a newly acquired fun hobby for me. In the past, I've enjoyed the role as a reader. However, recently, I have learned I absolutely love taking on the creative role as the writer. Something about determining how the story will play out intrigues me to no end. My husband claims that it's because I like to control things—in a way he's right!

By day, I run around from appointment to appointment wearing many hats including, mom, wife, part-time graphic designer, blogger, networker, social media stalker, student, business owner, and book boyfriend hunter (It's actually a thing—complete with pink camo. I lurk around the internet "researching" pictures of hot guys that fit the profile of whatever book boyfriend I'm reading or writing about).

I guess you can blame my obsession with books on my lovely grandmother whom is quite possibly my favorite person on the planet. At an early age, she took me to the Half-Priced bookstore each weekend and allowed me to choose a book. Every single time, she caved when I begged for two. Without her encouragement, I wouldn't have been able to cope during some hard times without my beloved books.

Currently, I am finishing up my college degree that has taken me forever to complete. It's just on the list of my many "bucket-list" goals that I subject myself to.

Most days, you can find me firmly planted in front of my computer. It's my life. If the world ever loses power, I'd be one of the first to die—of boredom! But, I guess as long as I have books and a light, I might just survive.

Looking forward, you can expect to see two more novels in the Breaking the Rules Series. I'm nearly finished with the third. Also, I have a standalone novel that will be released soon as well.

This writing experience has been a blast and I've met some really fabulous people along the way. I hope my readers enjoy reading my stories as much as I do writing them. I look forward to connecting with you all!

https://www.facebook.com/authorkwebster

http://authorkwebster.wordpress.com/

https://twitter.com/KristiWebster

kristi@authorwebster.com

https://www.goodreads.com/user/show/10439773-k-webster

http://instagram.com/kristiwebster

Made in the USA
Lexington, KY
04 December 2014